THE HAWK'S HEAD

"You have led me to treasure," muttered Yakub Khan, his naked sword gleaming in the dim light from the jeweled idol. "And now your usefulness is done."

"Wait!" cried Yar Muhammed. He picked up O'Donnell's scimitar from the floor, staring at the hawk's head that formed the hilt. "This is the sword of him who saved me from torture at the risk of his own life! His face was covered, as now, but I remember the hawk's head on his hilt. This man is the False Kurd!"

"Be silent," Yakub Khan snarled. "He is a god-thief, and we must prepare a god-thief's death!"

SWORDS OF SHAHRAZAR
ROBERT E. HOWARD

A BERKLEY MEDALLION BOOK
published by
BERKLEY PUBLISHING CORPORATION

Glenn Lord
P.O. Box 775
Pasadena, Texas 77501

SBN 425-03709-6

BERKLEY MEDALLION BOOKS are published by
Berkley Publishing Corporation
200 Madison Avenue
New York, N. Y. 10016

BERKLEY MEDALLION BOOK ® TM 757,375

Printed in the United States of America

Berkley Medallion Edition, MARCH, 1978

ACKNOWLEDGMENTS

The Treasures of Tartary, copyright 1934 by Metropolitan Magazines, Inc. for *Thrilling Adventures,* January 1935.

Swords of Shahrazar, copyright 1934 by Street & Smith Publications, Inc. for *Top-Notch,* October 1934.

The Curse of the Crimson God, copyright 1975 by Glenn Lord.

The Brazen Peacock, copyright 1975 by Glenn Lord for *REH: Lone Star Fictioneer,* Vol. 1, No. 3 (Fall 1975).

The Black Bear Bites, copyright 1973 by Harry O. Morris, Jr. and Edward P. Berglund for *From Beyond the Dark Gateway,* April 1974.

Contents

The Treasures of
Tartary

CHAPTER I

KEY TO THE TREASURE

It was not mere impulsiveness that sent Kirby O'Donnell into the welter of writhing limbs and whickering blades that loomed so suddenly in the semi-darkness ahead of him. In that dark alley of Forbidden Shahrazar it was no light act to plunge headlong into a nameless brawl; and O'Donnell, for all his Irish love of a fight, was not disposed thoughtlessly to jeopardize his secret mission.

But the glimpse of a scarred, bearded face swept from his mind all thought and emotion save a crimson wave of fury. He acted instinctively.

Full into the midst of the flailing group, half-seen by the light of a distant cresset, O'Donnell leaped, *kindhjal* in hand. He was dimly aware that one man was fighting three or four others, but all his attention was fixed on a single tall gaunt form, dim in the shadows. His long, narrow, curved blade licked venomously at this figure, ploughing through cloth, bringing a yelp as the edge sliced skin. Something crashed down on O'Donnell's head, gun butt or bludgeon, and he reeled, his eyes full of sparks, and closed with someone he could not see.

His groping hand locked on a chain that encircled a bull neck, and with a straining gasp he ripped upward and felt his keen *kindhjal* slice through cloth, skin and belly muscles. An agonized groan burst from his victim's lips, and blood gushed sickeningly over O'Donnell's hand.

Through a blur of clearing sight, the American saw a broad bearded face away from him—not the face he had seen before. The next instant he had leaped clear of the dying man, and was slashing at the shadowy forms about him. An instant of flickering steel, and then the figures were running fleetly up the alley. O'Donnell, springing in pursuit, his hot blood lashed to murderous fury, tripped over a writhing form and fell headlong. He rose, cursing, and was aware of a man near him, panting heavily. A tall man, with a long curved blade in hand. Three forms lay in the mud of the alley.

"Come, my friend, whoever you are!" the tall man panted in *Turki.* "They have fled, but they will return with others. Let us go!"

O'Donnell made no reply. Temporarily accepting the alliance into which chance had cast him, he followed the tall stranger who ran down the winding alley with the sure foot of familiarity. Silence held them until they emerged from a low dark arch, where a tangle of alleys debouched upon a broad square, vaguely lighted by small fires about which groups of turbaned men squabbled and brewed tea. A reek of unwashed bodies mingled with the odors of horses and camels. None noticed the two men standing in the shadow made by the angle of the mud wall.

O'Donnell looked at the stranger, seeing a tall slim

man with thin dark features. Under his *khalat* which
was draggled and darkly splashed, showed the silver-
heeled boots of a horseman. His turban was awry, and
though he had sheathed his scimitar, blood clotted the
hilt and the scabbard mouth.

The keen black eyes took in every detail of the
American's appearance, but O'Donnell did not flinch.
His disguise had stood the test too many times for him
to doubt its effectiveness.

The American was somewhat above medium height,
leanly built, but with broad shoulders and corded
sinews which gave him a strength out of all proportion
to his weight. He was a hard-woven mass of wiry
muscles and steel string nerves, combining the wolf-
trap coordination of a natural fighter with a berserk
fury resulting from an overflowing nervous energy.
The *kindhjal* in his girdle and the scimitar at his hip
were as much a part of him as his hands.

He wore the Kurdish boots, vest and girdled *khalat*
like a man born to them. His keen features, burned to
bronze by desert suns, were almost as dark as those of
his companion.

"Tell me thy name," requested the other. "I owe my
life to thee."

"I am Ali el Ghazi, a Kurd," answered O'Donnell.

No hint of suspicion shadowed the other's countenance. Under the coiffed Arab *kafiyeh* O'Donnell's
eyes blazed lambent blue, but blue eyes were not at all
unknown among the warriors of the Iranian highlands.

The Turk lightly and swiftly touched the hawk-
headed pommel of O'Donnell's scimitar.

"I will not forget," he promised. "I will know thee
wherever we meet again. Now it were best we separated
and went far from this spot, for men with knives will be
seeking me—and thou too, for aiding me." And like a

shadow he glided among the camels and bales and was gone.

O'Donnell stood silently for an instant, one ear cocked back toward the alley, the other absently taking in the sounds of the night. Somewhere a thin wailing voice sang to a twanging native lute. Somewhere else a feline-like burst of profanity marked the progress of a quarrel. O'Donnell breathed deep with contentment, despite the grim Hooded Figure that stalked forever at his shoulder, and the recent rage that still seethed in his veins. This was the real heart of the East, the East which had long ago stolen his heart and led him to wander afar from his own people.

He realized that he still gripped something in his left hand, and he lifted it to the flickering light of a nearby fire. It was a length of gold chain, one of its massy links twisted and broken. From it depended a curious plaque of beaten gold, somewhat larger than a silver dollar, but oval rather than round. There was no ornament, only a boldly carven inscription which O'Donnell, with all his Eastern lore, could not decipher.

He knew that he had torn the chain from the neck of the man he had killed in that black alley, but he had no idea as to its meaning. Slipping it into his broad girdle, he strode across the square, walking with the swagger of a nomadic horseman that was so natural to him.

Leaving the square he strode down a narrow street, the overhanging balconies of which almost touched one another. It was not late. Merchants in flowing silk robes sat cross-legged before their booths, extolling the quality of their goods—Mosul silk, matchlocks from Herat, edged weapons from India, and seed pearls from Baluchistan, Hawk-like Afghans and weapon-girdled Uzbeks jostled him. Lights streamed through silk-covered windows overhead, and the light silvery laughter of women rose above the noise of barter and dispute.

There was a tingle in the realization that he, Kirby O'Donnell, was the first Westerner ever to set foot in Forbidden Shahrazar, tucked away in a nameless valley not many days' journey from where the Afghan mountains swept down into the steppes of the Turkomans. As a wandering Kurd, traveling with a caravan from Kabul he had come, staking his life against the golden lure of a treasure beyond men's dreams.

In the bazaars and *serais* he had heard a tale: To Shaibar Khan, the Uzbek chief who had made himself master of Shahrazar, the city had given up its ancient secret. The Uzbek had found the treasure hidden there so long ago by Muhammad Shah, king of Khuwarezm, the Land of the Throne of Gold, when his empire fell before the Mongols.

O'Donnell was in Shahrazar to steal that treasure; and he did not change his plans because of the bearded face he had recognized in the alley—the face of an old and hated enemy. Yar Akbar the Afridi, traitor and murderer.

O'Donnell turned from the street and entered a narrow arched gate which stood open as if in invitation. A narrow stair went up from a small court to a balcony. This he mounted, guided by the tinkle of a guitar and a plaintive voice singing in *Pushtu*.

He entered a room whose latticed casement overhung the street, and the singer ceased her song to greet him and make a half-mocking salaam with a lithe flexing of supple limbs. He replied, and deposited himself on a divan. The furnishings of the room were not elaborate, but they were costly. The garments of the woman who watched interestedly were of silk, her satin vest sewn with seed pearls. Her dark eyes, over the filmy *yasmaq,* were lustrous and expressive, the eyes of a Persian.

"Would my lord have food—and wine?" she inquired; and O'Donnell signified assent with the lordly gesture of a Kurdish swashbuckler who is careful not to seem too courteous to any woman, however famed in intrigue she may be. He had come there not for food and drink, but because he had heard in the bazaars that news of many kinds blew on the winds through the house of Ayisha, where men from far and near came to drink her wine and listen to her songs.

She served him, and, sinking down on cushions near him, watched him eat and drink. O'Donnell's appetite was not feigned. Many lean days had taught him to eat when and where he could. Ayisha seemed to him more like a curious child than an intriguing woman, evincing so much interest over a wandering Kurd, but he knew that she was weighing him carefully behind her guileless stare, as she weighed all men who came into her house.

In that hot-bed of plot and ambitions, the wandering stranger today might be the Amir of Afghanistan or the Shah of Persia tomorrow—or the morrow might see his headless body dangling as a feast for the birds.

"You have a good sword," said she. He involuntarily touched the hilt. It was an Arab blade, long, lean, curved like the crescent moon, with a brass hawk's head for a pommel.

"It has cut many a Turkoman out of the saddle," he boasted, with his mouth full, carrying out his character. Yet it was no empty boast.

"Hai!" She believed him and was impressed. She rested her chin on her small fists and gazed up at him, as if his dark, hawk-like face had caught her fancy.

"The Khan needs swords like yours," she said.

"The Khan has many swords," he retorted, gulping wine loudly.

"No more than he will need if Orkhan Bahadur comes against him," she prophesied.

"I have heard of this Orkhan," he replied. And so he had; who in Central Asia had not heard of the daring and valorous Turkoman chief who defied the power of Moscow and had cut to pieces a Russian expedition sent to subdue him? "In the bazaars they say the Khan fears him."

That was a blind venture. Men did not speak of Shaibar Khan's fears openly.

Ayisha laughed. "Who does the Khan fear? Once the Amir sent troops to take Shahrazar, and those who lived were glad to flee! Yet if any man lives who could storm the city, Orkhan Bahadur is that man. Only tonight the Uzbeks were hunting his spies through the alleys."

O'Donnell remembered the Turkish accent of the stranger he had unwittingly aided. It was quite possible that the man was a Turkoman spy.

As he pondered this, Ayisha's sharp eyes discovered the broken end of the gold chain dangling from his girdle, and with a gurgle of delight she snatched it forth before he could stop her. Then with a squeal she dropped it as if it were hot, and prostrated herself in wriggling abasement among the cushions.

He scowled and picked up the trinket.

"Woman, what are you about?" he demanded.

"Your pardon, lord!" She clasped her hands, but her fear seemed more feigned than real; her eyes sparkled. "I did not know it was *the* token. *Aie,* you have been making game of me—asking me things none could know better than yourself. Which of the Twelve are you?"

"You babble as bees hum!" He scowled, dangling the pendant before her eyes. "You speak as one of knowledge, when, by Allah, you know not the meaning of this thing."

"Nay, but I do!" she protested. "I have seen such emblems before on the breasts of the *emirs* of the Inner Chamber. I know that it is a *talsmin* greater than the seal of the Amir, and the wearer comes and goes at will in or out of the Shining Palace."

"But why, wench, why?" he growled impatiently.

"Nay, I will whisper what you know so well," she answered, kneeling beside him. Her breath came soft as the sighing of the distant night wind. "It is the symbol of a Guardian of the Treasure!"

She fell away from him laughing. "Have I not spoken truly?"

He did not at once reply. His brain was dizzy, the blood pounding madly in his veins.

"Say nothing of this," he said at last, rising. "Your life upon it." And casting her a handful of coins at random, he hurried down the stair and into the street. He realized that his departure was too abrupt, but he was too dizzy, with the realization of what had fallen into his hands, for an entirely placid course of action.

The treasure! In his hand he held what well might be the key to it—at least a key into the palace, to gain entrance into which he had racked his brain ever since coming to Shahrazar. His visit to Ayisha had borne fruit beyond his wildest dreams.

CHAPTER II

THE UNHOLY PLAN

Doubtless in Muhammad Shah's day the Shining Palace deserved its name; even now it preserved some of its former splendor. It was separated from the rest of the city by a thick wall, and at the great gate there always stood a guard of Uzbeks with Lee-Enfield rifles, and girdles bristling with knives and pistols.

Shaibar Khan had an almost superstitious terror of accidental gunfire, and would allow only edged weapons to be brought into the palace. But his warriors were armed with the best rifles that could be smuggled into the Hills.

There was a limit to O'Donnell's audacity. There might be men on guard at the main gates who knew by sight all the *emirs* of the symbol. He made his way to a small side gate, through a loop-hole in which, at his imperious call, there peered a black man with the wizened features of a mute. O'Donnell had fastened the broken links together and the chain now looped his corded neck. He indicated the plaque which rested on the silk of his *khalat;* and with a deep salaam, the black man opened the gate.

O'Donnell drew a deep breath. He was in the heart of the lion's lair now, and he dared not hesitate or pause to deliberate. He found himself in a garden which gave on to an open court surrounded by arches supported on marble pillars. He crossed the court meeting no one. On the opposite side a grim-looking Uzbek, leaning on a spear, scanned him narrowly but said nothing. O'Donnell's skin crawled as he strode past the somber warrior, but the man merely stared curiously at the gold oval gleaming against the Kurdish vest.

O'Donnell found himself in a corridor whose walls were decorated by a gold frieze, and he went boldly on, seeing only soft-footed slaves who took no heed of him. As he passed into another corridor, broader and hung with velvet tapestries, his heart leaped into his mouth.

It was a tall slender man in long fur-trimmed robes and a silk turban who glided from an archway doorway and halted him. The man had the pale oval face of a Persian, with a black pointed beard, and dark shadowed eyes. As with the others his gaze sought first the *talsmin* on O'Donnell's breast—the token, undoubtedly, of a servitor beyond suspicion.

"Come with me!" snapped the Persian. "I have work for you." And vouchsafing no further enlightenment, he stalked down the corridor as if expecting O'Donnell to follow without question; which, indeed, the American did, believing that such would have been the action of the genuine Guardian of the Treasure. He knew this Persian was Ahmed Pasha, Shaibar Khan's vizir; he had seen him riding along the streets with the royal house troops.

The Persian led the way into a small domed chamber, without windows, the walls hung with thick tapestries. A small bronze lamp lighted it dimly. Ahmed Pasha drew aside the hangings, directly behind a heap of cushions, and disclosed a hidden alcove.

"Stand there with drawn sword," he directed. Then he hesitated. "Can you speak or understand any Frankish tongue?" he demanded. The false Kurd shook his head.

"Good!" snapped Ahmed Pasha. "You are here to watch, not to listen. Our lord does not trust the man he is to meet here—alone. You are stationed behind the spot where this man will sit. Watch him like a hawk. If he makes a move against the Khan, cleave his skull. If harm comes to our prince, you shall be flayed alive." He paused, glared an instant, then snarled:

"And hide that emblem, fool! Shall the whole world know you are an *emir* of the Treasure?"

"Hearkening and obedience, *ya khawand,*" mumbled O'Donnell, thrusting the symbol inside his garments. Ahmed jerked the tapestries together, and left the chamber. O'Donnell glanced through a tiny opening, waiting for the soft pad of the vizir's steps to fade away before he should glide out and take up again his hunt for the treasure.

But before he could move, there was a low mutter of voices, and two men entered the chamber from opposite sides. One bowed low and did not venture to seat himself until the other had deposited his fat body on the cushions, and indicated permission.

O'Donnell knew that he looked on Shaibar Khan, once the terror of the Kirghiz steppes, and now lord of Shahrazar. The Uzbek had the broad powerful build of his race, but his thick limbs were soft from easy living. His eyes held some of their old restless fire, but the muscles of his face seemed flabby, and his features were lined and purpled with debauchery. And there seemed something else—a worried, haunted look, strange in that son of reckless nomads. O'Donnell wondered if the possession of the treasure was weighing on his mind.

The other man was slender, dark, his garments plain beside the gorgeous ermine-trimmed *kaftan,* pearl-sewn girdle and green, emerald-crested turban of the Khan.

This stranger plunged at once into conversation, low-voiced but animated and urgent. He did most of the talking, while Shaibar Khan listened, occasionally interjecting a question, or a grunt of gratification. The Khan's weary eyes began to blaze, and his pudgy hands knotted as if they gripped again the hilt of the blade which had carved his way to power.

And Kirby O'Donnell forgot to curse the luck which held him prisoner while precious time drifted by. Both men spoke a tongue the American had not heard in years—a European language. And scanning closely the slim dark stranger, O'Donnell admitted himself baffled. If the man were, as he suspected, a European disguised as an Oriental, then O'Donnell knew he had met his equal in masquerade.

For it was European politics he talked, European politics that lay behind the intrigues of the East. He spoke of war and conquest, and vast hordes rolling down the Khyber Pass into India; to complete the overthrow, said the dark slender man, of a rule outworn.

He promised power and honors to Shaibar Khan, and O'Donnell, listening, realized that the Uzbek was but a pawn in his game, no less than those others he mentioned. The Khan, narrow of vision, saw only a mountain kingdom for himself, reaching down into the plains of Persia and India, and backed by European guns—not realizing those same guns could just as easily overwhelm him when the time was ripe.

But O'Donnell, with his western wisdom, read behind the dark stranger's words, and recognized there a plan of imperial dimensions, and the plot of a European power to seize half of Asia. And the first move in that game was to be the gathering of warriors by Shaibar Khan. How? With the treasure of Khuwarezm! With it he could buy all the swords of Central Asia.

So the dark man talked and the Uzbek listened like an old wolf who harks to the trampling of the musk oxen in the snow. O'Donnell listened, his blood freezing as the dark man casually spoke of invasions and massacres; and as the plot progressed and became more plain in detail, more monstrous and ruthless in conception, he trembled with a mad urge to leap from his cover and slash and hack both these bloody devils into pieces with the scimitar that quivered in his nervous grasp. Only a sense of self-preservation stayed him from this madness; and presently Shaibar Khan concluded the audience and left the chamber, followed by the dark stranger. O'Donnell saw this one smile furtively, like a man who has victory in his grasp.

O'Donnell started to draw aside the curtain, when Ahmed Pasha came padding into the chamber. It occurred to the American that it would be better to let the vizir find him at his post. But before Ahmed could speak, or draw aside the curtain, there sounded a rapid pattering of bare feet in the corridor outside, and a man burst into the room, wild eyed and panting. At the sight of him a red mist wavered across O'Donnell's sight. It was Yar Akbar!

CHAPTER III

WOLF PACK

The Afridi fell on his knees before Ahmed Pasha. His garments were tattered; blood seeped from a broken tooth and clotted his straggly beard.

"Oh, master," he panted, "the dog has escaped!"

"Escaped!" The vizir rose to his full height, his face convulsed with passion. O'Donnell thought that he would strike down the Afridi, but his arm quivered, fell by his side.

"Speak!" The Persian's voice was dangerous as the hiss of a cobra.

"We hedged him in a dark alley," Yar Akbar babbled. "He fought like *Shaitan*. Then others came to his aid—a whole nest of Turkomans, we thought, but mayhap it was but one man. He too was a devil! He slashed my side—see the blood! For hours since we have hunted them, but found no trace. *He* is over the wall and gone!" In his agitation Yar Akbar plucked at a chain about his neck; from it depended an oval like that held by O'Donnell. The American realized that Yar Akbar, too, was an *emir* of the Treasure. The Afridi's eyes burned like a wolf's in the gloom, and his voice sank.

"He who wounded me slew Othman," he whispered fearfully, "and despoiled him of the *talsmin!*"

"Dog!" The vizir's blow knocked the Afridi sprawling. Ahmed Pasha was livid. "Call the other *emirs* of the Inner Chamber, swiftly!"

Yar Akbar hastened into the corridor, and Ahmed Pasha called:

"Ohe! you who hide behind the hangings—come forth!" There was no reply, and pale with sudden suspicion, Ahmed drew a curved dagger and with a pantherish spring tore the tapestry aside. The alcove was empty.

As he glared in bewilderment, Yar Akbar ushered into the chamber as unsavory a troop of ruffians as a man might meet, even in the Hills: Uzbeks, Afghans, Gilzais, Pathans, scarred with crime and old in wickedness. Ahmed Pasha counted them swiftly. With Yar Akbar there were eleven.

"Eleven," he muttered. "And dead Othman makes twelve. All these men are known to you, Yar Akbar?"

"My own head on it!" swore the Afridi. "These be all true men."

Ahmed clutched his beard.

"Then, by God, the One True God," he groaned, "that Kurd I set to guard the Khan was a spy and a traitor." And at that moment a shriek and a clash of steel re-echoed through the palace.

When O'Donnell heard Yar Akbar gasping out his tale to the vizir, he knew the game was up. He did not believe that the alcove was a blind niche in the wall; and, running swift and practiced hands over the panels, he found and pressed a hidden catch. An instant before Ahmed Pasha tore aside the tapestry, the American wriggled his lean body through the opening and found himself in a dimly lighted chamber on the other side of the wall. A black slave dozed on his haunches, unmindful of the blade that hovered over his ebony neck, as O'Donnell glided across the room and through a curtained doorway.

He found himself back in the corridor into which one door of the audience chamber opened, and

crouching among the curtains, he saw Yar Akbar come
up the hallway with his villainous crew. He saw, too,
that they had come up a marble stair at the end of the
hall.

His heart leaped. In that direction, undoubtedly, lay
the treasure—now supposedly unguarded. As soon as
the *emirs* vanished into the audience chamber where
the vizir waited, O'Donnell ran swiftly and recklessly
down the corridor.

But even as he reached the stairs, a man sitting on
them sprang up, brandishing a *tulwar*. A black slave,
evidently left there with definite orders, for the sight of
the symbol on O'Donnell's breast did not halt him.
O'Donnell took a desperate chance, gambling his
speed against the cry that rose in the thick black throat.

He lost. His scimitar licked through the massive
neck and the Soudani rolled down the stairs, spurting
blood. But his yell had rung to the roof.

And at that yell the *emirs* of the gold came headlong
out of the audience chamber, giving tongue like a pack
of wolves. They did not need Ahmed's infuriated shriek
of recognition and command. They were men picked
for celerity of action as well as courage, and it seemed
to O'Donnell that they were upon him before the
negro's death yell had ceased to echo.

He met the first attacker, a hairy Pathan, with a long
lunge that sent his scimitar point through the thick
throat even as the man's broad *tulwar* went up for a
stroke. Then a tall Uzbek swung his heavy blade like a
butcher's cleaver. No time to parry; O'Donnell caught
the stroke near his own hilt, and his knees bent under
the impact.

But the next instant the *kindhjal* in his left hand
ripped through the Uzbek's entrails, and with a

powerful heave of his whole body, O'Donnell hurled the dying man against those behind him, bearing them back with him. Then O'Donnell wheeled and ran, his eyes blazing defiance of the death that whickered at his back.

Ahead of him another stair led up. O'Donnell reached it one long bound ahead of his pursuers, gained the steps and wheeled, all in one motion, slashing down at the heads of the pack that came clamoring after him.

Shaibar Khan's broad pale face peered up at the mêlée from the curtains of an archway, and O'Donnell was grateful to the Khan's obsessional fear that had barred firearms from the palace. Otherwise, he would already have been shot down like a dog. He himself had no gun; the pistol with which he had started the adventure had slipped from its holster somewhere on that long journey, and lay lost among the snows of the Himalayas.

No matter; he had never yet met his match with cold steel. But no blade could long have held off the ever increasing horde that swarmed up the stair at him.

He had the advantage of position, and they could not crowd past him on the narrow stair; their very numbers hindered them. His flesh crawled with the fear that others would come down the stair and take him from behind, but none came. He retreated slowly, plying his dripping blades with berserk frenzy. A steady stream of taunts and curses flowed from his lips, but even in his fury he spoke in the tongues of the East, and not one of his assailants realized that the madman who opposed them was anything but a Kurd.

He was bleeding from a dozen flesh cuts, when he reached the head of the stairs which ended in an open trap. Simultaneously the wolves below him came clambering up to drag him down. One gripped his knees, another was hewing madly at his head. The others howled below them, unable to get at their prey.

O'Donnell stooped beneath the sweep of a *tulwar* and his scimitar split the skull of the wielder. His *kindhjal* he drove through the breast of the man who clung to his knees, and kicking the clinging body away from him, he reeled up through the trap. With frantic energy, he gripped the heavy iron-bound door and slammed it down, falling across it in semi-collapse.

The splintering of wood beneath him warned him and he rolled clear just as a steel point crunched up through the door and quivered in the starlight. He found and shot the bolt, and then lay prostrate, panting for breath. How long the heavy wood would resist the attacks from below he did not know.

He was on a flat-topped roof, the highest part of the palace. Rising, he stumbled over to the nearest parapet, and looked down, on to lower roofs. He saw no way to get down. He was trapped.

It was the darkness just before dawn. He was on a higher level than the walls or any of the other houses in Shahrazar. He could dimly make out the sheer of the great cliffs which flanked the valley in which Shahrazar stood, and he saw the starlight's pale glimmer on the slim river which trickled past the massive walls. The valley ran southeast and northwest.

And suddenly the wind, whispering down from the north, brought a burst of crackling reports. Shots? He stared northwestward, toward where, he knew, the valley pitched upward, narrowing to a sheer gut, and a mud-walled village dominated the pass. He saw a dull red glow against the sky. Again came reverberations.

Somewhere in the streets below sounded a frantic clatter of flying hoofs that halted before the palace gate. There was silence then, in which O'Donnell heard the splintering blows on the trap door, and the heavy breathing of the men who struck them. Then suddenly they ceased as if the attackers had dropped dead; utter silence attended a shrilling voice, indistinct through distance and muffling walls. A wild clamor burst forth in the streets below; men shouted, women screamed.

No more blows fell on the trap. Instead there were noises below—the rattle of arms, tramp of men, and a voice that held a note of hysteria shouting orders.

O'Donnell heard the clatter of galloping horses, and saw torches moving through the streets, toward the northwestern gate. In the darkness up the valley he saw orange jets of flame and heard the unmistakable reports of firearms.

Shrugging his shoulders, he sat down in an angle of the parapet, his scimitar across his knees. And there weary Nature asserted itself, and in spite of the clamor below him, and the riot in his blood, he slept.

CHAPTER IV

FURIOUS BATTLE!

He did not sleep long, for dawn was just stealing whitely over the mountains when he awoke. Rifles were cracking all around, and crouching at the parapet, he saw the reason. Shahrazar was besieged by warriors in sheepskin coats and fur *kalpaks*. Herds of their horse grazed just beyond rifle fire, and the warriors themselves were firing from every rock and tree. Numbers of them were squirming along the half dry river bed, among the willows, sniping at the men on the walls, who gave back their fire.

The Turkomans of Orkhan Bahadur! That blaze in the darkness told of the fate of the village that guarded the pass. Turks seldom made night raids; but Orkhan was nothing if not original.

The Uzbeks manned the walls, and O'Donnell believed he could make out the bulky shape and crested turban of Shaibar Khan among a cluster of peacock-clad nobles. And as he gazed at the turmoil in the streets below, the belief grew that every available Uzbek in the city was on the walls. This was no mere raid; it was a tribal war of extermination.

O'Donnell's Irish audacity rose like heady wine in his veins, and he tore aside the splintered door and gazed down the stairs. The bodies still lay on the steps, stiff and unseeing. No living human met his gaze as he stole down the stairs, scimitar in hand. He gained the broad corridor, and still he saw no one. He hurried down the stair whereon he had slain the black slave, and reached a broad chamber with a single tapestried door.

There was the sudden crash of a musket; a spurt of flame stabbed at him. The ball whined past him and he covered the space with a long leap, grappled a snarling, biting figure behind the tapestry and dragged it into the open. It was Ahmed Pasha.

"Accursed one!" The vizir fought like a mad dog. "I guessed you would come skulking here—Allah's curse on the *hashish* that has made my hand unsteady—"

His dagger girded through O'Donnell's garments,

drawing blood. Under his silks the Persian's muscles were like taut wires. Employing his superior weight, the American hurled himself hard against the other, driving the vizir's head back against the stone wall with a stunning crack. As the Persian relaxed with a groan, O'Donnell's left hand wrenched from his grasp and lurched upward, and the keen *kindhjal* encountered flesh and bone.

The American lifted the still twitching corpse and thrust it behind the tapestry, hiding it as best he could. A bunch of keys at the dead man's girdle caught his attention, and they were in his hand as he approached the curtained door.

The heavy teakwood portal, bound in arabesqued copper, would have resisted any onslaught short of artillery. A moment's fumbling with the massive keys, and O'Donnell found the right one. He passed into a narrow corridor dimly lighted by some obscure means. The walls were of marble, the floor of mosaics. It ended at what seemed to be a blank carven wall, until O'Donnell saw a thin crack in the marble.

Through carelessness or haste, the secret door had been left partly open. O'Donnell heard no sound, and was inclined to believe that Ahmed Pasha had remained to guard the treasure alone. He gave the vizir credit for wit and courage.

O'Donnell pulled open the door—a wide block of marble revolving on a pivot—and halted short, a low cry escaping his lips. He had come full upon the treasure of Khuwarezm, and the sight stunned him!

The dim light must have come through hidden interstices in the colored dome of the circular chamber in which he stood. It illumined a shining pyramidal heap upon a dais in the center of the floor, a platform

that was a great round slab of pure jade. And on that
jade gleamed tokens of wealth beyond the dreams of
madness. The foundations of the pile consisted of
blocks of virgin gold and upon them lay, rising to a
pinnacle of blazing splendor, ingots of hammered
silver, ornaments of golden enamel, wedges of jade,
pearls of incredible perfection, inlaid ivory, diamonds
that dazzled the sight, rubies like clotted blood,
emeralds like drops of green fire, pulsing sapphires—
O'Donnell's senses refused to accept the wonder of
what he saw. Here, indeed, was wealth sufficient to buy
every sword in Asia. A sudden sound brought him
about. Someone was coming down the corridor
outside, someone who labored for breath and ran
staggeringly. A quick glance around, and O'Donnell
slipped behind the rich gilt-worked arras which
masked the walls. A niche where, perhaps, had stood
an idol in the old pagan days, admitted his lean body,
and he gazed through a slit cut in the velvet.

It was Shaibar Khan who came into the chamber.
The Khan's garments were torn and splashed darkly.
He stared at his treasure with haunted eyes, and he
groaned. Then he called for Ahmed Pasha.

One man came, but it was not the vizir who lay dead
in the outer corridor. It was Yar Akbar, crouching like
a great grey wolf, beard bristling in his perpetual snarl.

"Why was the treasure left unguarded?" demanded
Shaibar Khan petulantly. "Where is Ahmed Pasha?"

"He sent us on the wall," answered Yar Akbar,
hunching his shoulders in servile abasement. "He said
he would guard the treasure himself."

"No matter!" Shaibar Khan was shaking like a man
with an ague. "We are lost. The people have risen
against me and opened the gates to that devil Orkhan

Bahadur. His Turkomans are cutting down my Uzbeks in the streets. But he shall not have the treasure. See ye that golden bar that juts from the wall, like a sword hilt from the scabbard? I have but to pull that, and the treasure falls into the subterranean river which runs below this palace, to be lost forever to the sight of men. Yar Akbar, I give you a last command—pull that bar!"

Yar Akbar moaned and wrung his beard, but his eyes were red as a wolf's, and he turned his ear continually toward the outer door.

"Nay, lord, ask of me anything but that!"

"Then I will do it!" Shaibar Khan moved toward the bar, reached out his hand to grasp it. With a snarl of a wild beast, Yar Akbar sprang on his back, grunting as he struck. O'Donnell saw the point of the Khyber knife spring out of Shaibar Khan's silk-clad breast, as the Uzbek chief threw wide his arms, cried out chokingly, and tumbled forward to the floor. Yar Akbar spurned the dying body with a vicious foot.

"Fool!" he croaked. "I will buy my life from Orkhan Bahadur. Aye, this treasure shall gain me much honor with him, now the other *emirs* are dead—"

He halted, crouching and glaring, the reddened knife quivering in his hairy fist. O'Donnell had swept aside the tapestry and stepped into the open. "Y'Allah!" ejaculated the Afridi. "The dog-Kurd!"

"Look more closely, Yar Akbar," answered O'Donnell grimly, throwing back his *kafiyeh* and speaking in English. "Do you not remember the Gorge of Izz ed din and the scout trapped there by your treachery? One man escaped, you dog of the Khyber."

Slowly a red flame grew in Yar Akbar's eyes.

"El Shirkuh!" he muttered, giving O'Donnell his Afghan name—the Mountain Lion. Then, with a howl

that rang to the domed roof, he launched himself
through the air, his three-foot knife gleaming.

O'Donnell did not move his feet. A supple twist of
his torso avoided the thrust, and the furiously driven
knife hissed between left arm and body, tearing his
khalat. At the same instant O'Donnell's left forearm
bent up and under the lunging arm that guided the
knife. Yar Akbar screamed, spat on the *kindhjal's*
narrow blade. Unable to halt his headlong rush, he
caromed bodily against O'Donnell, bearing him down.

They struck the floor together, and Yar Akbar, with
a foot of trenchant steel in his vitals, yet reared up,
caught O'Donnell's hair in a fierce grasp, gasped a
curse, lifted his knife—and then his wild beast vitality
failed him, and with a convulsive shudder he rolled
clear and lay still in a spreading pool of blood.

O'Donnell rose and stared down at the bodies upon
the floor, then at the glittering heap on the jade slab.
His soul yearned to it with the fierce yearning that had
haunted him for years. Dared he take the desperate
chance of hiding it under the very noses of the invading
Turkomans? If he could, he might escape, to return
later, and bear it away. He had taken more desperate
chances before.

Across his mental vision flashed a picture of a slim
dark stranger who spoke a European tongue. It was
lure of the treasure which had led Orkhan Bahadur out
of his steppes; and the treasure in his hands would be as
dangerous as it was in the hands of Shaibar Khan. The
Power represented by the dark stranger could deal with
the Turkoman as easily as with the Uzbek.

No; one Oriental adventurer with that treasure was
as dangerous to the peace of Asia as another. He dared
not run the risk of Orkhan Bahadur finding that pile of

gleaming wealth—sweat suddenly broke out on O'Donnell's body as he realized, for once in his life, a driving power mightier than his own desire. The helpless millions of India were in his mind as, cursing sickly, he gripped the gold bar and heaved it!

With a grinding boom something gave way, the jade slab moved, turned, tilted and disappeared, and with it vanished, in a final iridescent burst of dazzling splendor, the treasure of Khuwarezm. Far below came a sullen splash, and the sound of waters roaring in the darkness; then silence, and where a black hole had gaped there showed a circular slab of the same substance as the rest of the floor.

O'Donnell hurried from the chamber. He did not wish to be found where the Turkomans might connect him with the vanishing of the treasure they had battled to win. Let them think, if they would, that Shaibar Khan and Yar Akbar had disposed of it somehow, and slain one another. As he emerged from the palace into an outer court, lean warriors in sheepskin *kaftans* and high fur caps were swarming in. Cartridge belts crossed on their breasts, and *yataghans* hung at their girdles. One of them lifted a rifle and took deliberate aim at O'Donnell.

Then it was struck aside, and a voice shouted:

"By Allah, it is my friend Ali el Ghazi!" There strode forward a tall man whose *kalpak* was of white lambskin, and whose *kaftan* was trimmed with ermine. O'Donnell recognized the man he had aided in the alley.

"I am Orkhan Bahadur!" exclaimed the chief with a ringing laugh. "Put up your sword, friend; Shahrazar is mine! The heads of the Uzbeks are heaped in the market square! When I fled from their swords last night, they little guessed my warriors awaited my coming in the mountains beyond the pass! Now I am prince of Shahrazar, and thou art my cup-companion. Ask what thou wilt, yea, even a share of the treasure of Khuwarezm—when we find it."

"When you find it!" O'Donnell mentally echoed, sheathing his scimitar with a Kurdish swagger. The American was something of a fatalist. He had come out of this adventure with his life at least, and the rest was in the hands of Allah.

"Alhamdolillah!" said O'Donnell, joining arms with his new cup-companion.

*Swords of
Shahrazar*

Kirby O'Donnell opened his chamber door and gazed out, his long keen-bladed *kindhjal* in his hand. Somewhere a cresset glowed fitfully, dimly lighting the broad hallway, flanked by thick columns. The spaces between these columns were black arched wells of darkness, where anything might be lurking.

Nothing moved within his range of vision. The great hall seemed deserted. But he knew that he had not merely dreamed that he heard the stealthy pad of bare feet outside his door, the stealthy sound of unseen hands trying the portal.

O'Donnell felt the peril that crawled unseen about him, the first white man ever to set foot in forgotten Shahrazar, the forbidden, age-old city brooding high among the Afghan mountains. He believed his disguise was perfect; as Ali el Ghazi, a wandering Kurd, he had entered Shahrazar, and as such he was a guest in the palace of its prince. But the furtive footfalls that had awakened him were a sinister portent.

He stepped out into the hall cautiously, closing the

door behind him. A single step he took—it was the swish of a garment that warned him. He whirled, quick as a cat, and saw, all in a split second, a great black body, hurtling at him from the shadows, the gleam of a plunging knife. And simultaneously he himself moved in a blinding blur of speed. A shift of his whole body avoided the stroke, and as the blade licked past, splitting only thin air, his *kindhjal,* driven with desperate energy, sank its full length in the black torso.

An agonized groan was choked by a rush of blood in the dusky throat. The Negro's knife rang on the marble floor, and the great black figure, checked in its headlong rush, swayed drunkenly and pitched forward. O'Donnell watched with his eyes as hard as flint as the would-be murderer shuddered convulsively and then lay still in a widening crimson pool.

He recognized the man, and as he stood staring down at his victim, a train of associations passed swiftly through his mind, recollections of past events crowding on a realization of his present situation.

Lure of treasure had brought O'Donnell in his disguise to forbidden Shahrazar. Since the days of Genghis Khan, Shahrazar had sheltered the treasure of the long-dead shahs of Khuwarezm. Many an adventurer had sought that fabled hoard, and many had died. But O'Donnell had found it—only to lose it.

Hardly had he arrived in Shahrazar when a band of marauding Turkomans, under their chief, Orkhan Bahadur, had stormed the city and captured it, slaying its prince, the Uzbek Shaibar Khan. And while the battle raged in the streets, O'Donnell had found the hidden treasure in a secret chamber, and his brain had reeled at its splendor. But he had been unable to bear it away, and he dared not leave it for Orkhan. The

emissary of an intriguing European power was in
Shahrazar, plotting to use that treasure to conquer
India. O'Donnell had done away with it forever. The
victorious Turkomans had searched for it in vain.

O'Donnell, as Ali el Ghazi, had once saved Orkhan
Bahadur's life, and the prince made the supposed Kurd
welcome in the palace. None dreamed of his connection with the disappearance of the hoard, unless—
O'Donnell stared somberly down at the figure on the
marble floor.

That man was Baber, a Soudani servant of
Suleiman Pasha, the emissary.

O'Donnell lifted his head and swept his gaze over
the black arches, the shadowy columns. Had he only
imagined that he heard movement back in the
darkness? Bending over quickly, he grasped the limp
body and heaved it on his shoulder—an act impossible
for a man with less steely thews—and started down the
hall. A corpse found before his door meant questions,
and the fewer questions O'Donnell had to answer the
better.

He went down the broad, silent hall and descended a
wide marble stair into swallowing gloom, like an
oriental demon carrying a corpse to hell; groped
through a tapestried door and down a short, black
corridor to a blank marble wall.

When he thrust against this with his foot, a section
swung inward, working on a pivot, and he entered a
circular, domed chamber with a marble floor and walls
hung with heavy gilt-worked tapestries, between which
showed broad golden-frieze work. A bronze lamp cast
a soft light, making the dome seem lofty and full of
shadows, while the tapestries were clinging squares of
velvet darkness.

This had been the treasure vault of Shaibar Khan, and why it was empty now, only Kirby O'Donnell could tell.

Lowering the black body with a gasp of relief, for the burden had taxed even his wiry thews to the utmost, he desposited it exactly on the great disk that formed the center of the marble floor. Then he crossed the chamber, seized a gold bar that seemed merely part of the ornamentation, and jerked it strongly. Instantly the great central disk revolved silently, revealing a glimpse of a black opening, into which the corpse tumbled. The sound of rushing water welled up from the darkness, and then the slab, swinging on its pivot, completed its revolution and the floor showed again a smooth unbroken surface.

But O'Donnell wheeled suddenly. The lamp burned low, filling the chamber with a lurid unreal light. In that light he saw the door open silently and a slim dark figure glide in.

It was a slender man with long nervous hands and an ivory oval of a face, pointed with a short black beard. His eyes were long and oblique, his garments dark, even his turban. In his hand a blue, snub-nosed revolver glinted dully.

"Suleiman Pasha!" muttered O'Donnell tensely.

He had never been able to decide whether this man was the Oriental he seemed, or a European in masquerade. Had the man penetrated his own disguise? The emissary's first words assured him that such was not the case.

"Ali el Ghazi," said Suleiman, "you have lost me a valuable servant, but you have told me a secret. None other knows the secret of that revolving slab. I did not, until I followed you, after you killed Baber, and watched you through the door, though I have suspected that this chamber was the treasure vault.

"I have suspected you—now I am certain. I know why the treasure has never been found. You disposed of it as you have disposed of Baber. You are cup-companion to Prince Orkhan Bahadur. But if I told him you cast away the treasure forever, do you suppose his friendship would prevail over his wrath?

"Keep back!" he warned. "I did not say that I would tell Orkhan. Why you threw away the treasure I cannot guess, unless it was because of fanatical loyalty to Shaibar Kahn."

He looked him over closely. "Face like a hawk, body of coiled steel springs," he murmured. "I can use you, my Kurdish swaggerer."

"How use me?" demanded O'Donnell.

"You can help me in the game I play with Orkhan Bahadur. The treasure is gone, but I can still use him, I and the *Feringis* who employ me. I will make him amir of Afghanistan and, after that, sultan of India."

"And the puppet of the *Feringis,*" grunted O'Donnell.

"What is that to thee?" Suleiman laughed. "Time is not to think. I will do the thinking; see thou to the enacting of my commands."

"I have not said that I would serve you," growled O'Donnell doggedly.

"You have no other choice," answered Suleiman calmly. "If you refuse, I will reveal to Orkhan that which I learned tonight, and he will have you flayed alive."

O'Donnell bent his head moodily. He was caught in a vise of circumstances. It had not been loyalty to Shaibar Kahn, as Suleiman thought, which had caused him to dump an emperor's ransom in gold and jewels into the subterranean river. He knew Suleiman plotted the overthrow of British rule in India and the massacre of the helpless millions. He knew that Orkhan Bahadur, a ruthless adventurer despite his friendship for the false Kurd, was a pliant tool in the emissary's hands. The treasure had been too potent a weapon to leave within their reach.

Suleiman was either a Russian or the Oriental tool of the Russians. Perhaps he, too, had secret ambitions. The Khuwarezm treasure had been a pawn in his game; but, even without it, a tool of the emissary's sitting on the throne of Shahrazar, was a living menace to the peace of India. So O'Donnell had remained in the city, seeking in every way to thwart Suleiman's efforts to dominate Orkhan Bahadur. And now he himself was trapped.

He lifted his head and stared murderously at the slim Oriental. "What do you wish me to do?" he muttered.

"I have a task for you," answered Suleiman. "An hour ago word came to me, by one of my secret agents, that the tribesmen of Khuruk had found an Englishman dying in the hills, with valuable papers upon him. I must have those papers. I sent the man on to Orkhan, while I dealt with you.

"But I have changed my plans in regard to you; you are more valuable to me alive than dead, since there is no danger of your opposing me in the future. Orkhan will desire those papers that the Englishman carried, for the man was undoubtedly a secret-service agent, and I will persuade the prince to send you with a troop of horsemen to secure them. And remember you are taking your real orders from me, not from Orkhan."

He stepped aside and motioned O'Donnell to precede him.

* * *

They traversed the short corridor, an electric torch in Suleiman's left hand playing its beam on his sullen, watchful companion, climbed the stair and went through the wide hall, thence along a winding corridor and into a chamber where Orkhan Bahadur stood near a gold-barred window which opened onto an arcaded court, which was just being whitened by dawn. The prince of Shahrazar was resplendent in satin and pearl-sewn velvet which did not mask the hard lines of his lean body.

His thin dark features lighted at the sight of his cup-companion, but O'Donnell reflected on the wolf that lurked ever below the surface of this barbaric chieftain, and how suddenly it could be unmasked, snarling and flame-eyed.

"Welcome, friends!" said the Turkoman, pacing the chamber restlessly. "I have heard a tale! Three days' ride to the southwest are the villages of Ahmed Shah, in the valley of Khuruk. Four days ago his men came upon a man dying in the mountains. He wore the garments of an Afghan, but in his delirium he revealed himself as an Englishman. When he was dead they searched him for loot and found certain papers which none of the dogs could read.

"But in his ravings he spoke of having been to Bowhara. It is in my mind that this *Feringi* was an English spy, returning to India with papers valuable to the *sirkar*. Perhaps the British would pay well for these papers, if they knew of them. It is my wish to possess them. Yet I dare not ride forth myself, nor send many men. Suppose the treasure was found in my absence? My own men would bar the gates against me."

"This is a matter for diplomacy rather than force," put in Suleiman Pasha smoothly. "Ali el Ghazi is crafty as well as bold. Send him with fifty men."

"Can thou do it, brother?" demanded Orkhan eagerly.

Suleiman's gaze burned into O'Donnell's soul. There was but one answer, if he wished to escape flaying steel and searing fire.

"Only in Allah is power," he muttered. "Yet I can attempt the thing."

"Mashallah!" exclaimed Orkhan. "Be ready to start within the hour. There is a Khurukzai in the *suk,* one Dost Shah, who is of Ahmed's clan, and will guide you. There is friendship between me and the men of Khuruk. Approach Ahmed Shah in peace and offer him gold for the papers, but not too much, lest his cupidity be roused. But I leave it to your own judgement. With fifty men there is no fear of the smaller clans between Shahrazar and Khuruk. I go now to choose the men to ride with you."

As soon as Orkhan left the chamber, Suleiman bent close to O'Donnell and whispered: "Secure the papers, but do not bring them to Orkhan! Pretend that you have lost them in the hills—anything—but bring them to *me.*"

"Orkhan will be angry and suspicious," objected O'Donnell.

"Not half as angry as he would be if he knew what became of the Khuwarezm treasure," retorted Suleiman. "Your only chance is to obey me. If your men return without you, saying you have fled away, be sure a hundred men will quickly be upon your trail—nor can you hope to win alone through these hostile, devil-haunted hills, anyway. Do not dare to return without the papers, if you do not wish to be denounced to Orkhan. Your life depends on your playing my game, Kurd!"

Playing Suleiman's "game" seemed to be the only thing to do, even three days later as O'Donnell, in his guise of the Kurdish swashbuckler, Ali el Ghazi, was riding along a trail that followed a ledgelike fold of rock ribbing a mile-wide cliff.

Just ahead of him a bony crowbait rode the Khurukzai guide, a hairy savage with a dirty white turban, and behind him strung out in single file fifty of Orkhan Bahadur's picked warriors. O'Donnell felt the pride of a good leader of fighting men as he glanced back at them. These were no stunted peasants, but tall, sinewy men with the pride and temper of hawks; nomads and sons of nomads, born to the saddle. They rode horses that were distinctive in that land of horsemen, and their rifles were modern repeaters.

"Listen!" It was the Khurukzai who halted, suddenly, lifting a hand in warning.

O'Donnell leaned forward, rising in the wide silver stirrups, turning his head slightly sidewise. A gust of wind whipped along the ledge, bearing with it the echoes of a series of sputtering reports.

The men behind O'Donnell heard it, too, and there was a creaking of saddles as they instinctively unslung rifles and hitched yataghan hilts forward.

"Rifles!" exclaimed Dost Shah. "Men are fighting in the hills."

"How far are we from Khuruk?" asked O'Donnell.

"An hour's ride," answered the Khurukzai, glancing at the mid-afternoon sun. "Beyond the corner of the cliff we can see the Pass of Akbar, which is the boundary of Ahmed Shah's territory. Khuruk is some miles beyond."

"Push on, then," said O'Donnell.

They moved on around the crag which jutted out like the prow of a ship, shutting off all view to the south. The path narrowed and sloped there, so the men dismounted and edged their way, leading the animals which grew half frantic with fear.

Ahead of them the trail broadened and sloped up to a fan-shaped plateau, flanked by rugged ridges. This plateau narrowed to a pass in a solid wall of rock hundreds of feet high; the pass was a triangular gash, and a stone tower in its mouth commanded the approach. There were men in the tower, and they were firing at other men who lay out on the plateau in a wide ragged crescent, concealed behind boulders and rocky ledges. But these were not all firing at the tower, as it presently became apparent.

Off to the left of the pass, skirting the foot of the cliffs, a ravine meandered. Men were hiding in this ravine, and O'Donnell quickly saw that they were trapped there. The men out on the plateau had cast a cordon around it and were working their way closer, shooting as they came. The men in the ravine fired back, and a few corpses were strewn among the rocks. But from the sound of the firing, there were only a few men in the gully, and the men in the tower could not come to their aid. It would have been suicide to try to cross that bullet-swept open space between the ravine and the pass mouth.

O'Donnell had halted his men at an angle of the cliff where the trail wound up toward the plateau, and had advanced with the Khurukzai guide part way up the incline.

"What does this mean?" he asked.

Dost Shah shook his head like one puzzled. "That is the Pass of Akbar," he said. "That tower is Ahmed Shah's. Sometimes the tribes come to fight us, and we shoot them from the tower. It can only be Ahmed's riflemen in the tower and in the ravine. But—"

He shook his head again, and having tied his horse to a straggling tamarisk, he went up the slope, craning his neck and hugging his rifle, while he muttered in his beard as if in uncertainty.

O'Donnell followed him to the crest where the trail bent over the rim of the plateau, but with more caution than the Khurukzai was showing. They were now within rifle range of the combatants, and bullets were whistling like hornets across the plateau.

O'Donnell could plainly make out the forms of the besiegers lying among the rocks that littered the narrow plain. Evidently they had not noticed him and the guide, and he did not believe they saw his men where he had stationed them in the shade of an overhanging crag. All their attention was fixed on the ravine, and they yelled with fierce exultation as a turban thrust above its rim fell back splashed with crimson. The men in the tower yelled with helpless fury.

"Keep your head down, you fool!" O'Donnell swore at Dost Shah, who was carelessly craning his long neck above a cluster of rocks.

"The men in the tower *must* be Ahmed's men," muttered Dost Shah uneasily. "Yes; it could not be otherwise, yet—Allah!" The last was an explosive yelp, and he sprang up like a madman, as if forgetting all caution in some other overwhelming emotion.

O'Donnell cursed and grabbed at him to pull him

down, but he stood brandishing his rifle, his tattered garments whipping in the wind like a demon of the hills.

"What devil's work is this?" he yelled. "That is not—those are not—"

His voice changed to a gasp as a bullet drilled him through the temple. He tumbled back to the ground and lay without motion.

"Now what was he going to say?" muttered O'Donnell, peering out over the rocks. "Was that a stray slug, or did somebody see him?"

He could not tell whether the shot came from the boulders or the tower. It was typical of hill warfare, the yells and shooting keeping up an incessant devil's din. One thing was certain: the cordon was gradually closing about the men trapped in the ravine. They were well hidden from the bullets, but the attackers were working so close that presently they could finish the job with a short swift rush and knife work at close quarters.

O'Donnell fell back down the incline, and coming to the eager Turkomans, spoke hurriedly: "Dost Shah is dead, but he has brought us to the borders of Ahmed Shah's territory. Those in the tower are Khurukzai, and these men attacking them have cut off some chief—probably Ahmed Shah himself—in that ravine. I judge that from the noise both sides are making. Then, they'd scarcely be taking such chances to slaughter a few common warriors. If we rescue him we shall have a claim on his friendship, and our task will be made easy, as Allah makes all things for brave men.

"The men attacking seem to me not to number more than a hundred men—twice our number, true, but there are circumstances in our favor, surprise, and the

fact that the men in the pass will undoubtedly sally out
if we create a diversion in the enemy's rear. At present
the Khurukzai are bottled in the pass. They cannot
emerge, any more than the raiders can enter in the teeth
of their bullets."

"We await orders," the men answered.

Turkomans have no love for Kurds, but the
horsemen knew that Ali el Ghazi was cup-companion
to their prince.

"Ten men to hold the horses!" he snapped. "The rest
follow me."

A few minutes later they were crawling after him up
the short slope. He lined them along the crest, seeing
that each man was sheltered among the boulders.

This took but a few minutes, but in that interim the
men crawling toward the ravine sprang to their feet and
tore madly across the intervening space, yelling like
blood-crazed wolves, their curved blades glittering in
the sun. Rifles spat from the gully and three of the
attackers dropped, and the men in the tower sent up an
awful howl and turned their guns desperately on the
charging mob. But the range at that angle was too
great.

Then O'Donnell snapped an order, and a withering
line of flame ran along the crest of the ridge. His men
were picked marksmen and understood the value of
volleys. Some thirty men were in the open, charging the
ravine. A full half of them went down struck from
behind, as if by some giant invisible fist. The others
halted, realizing that something was wrong; they
cringed dazedly, turning here and there, grasping their
long knives, while the bullets of the Turkomans took
further toll.

Then, suddenly, realizing that they were being
attacked from the rear, they dived screaming for cover.

The men in the tower, sensing reinforcements, sent up a wild shout and redoubled their fire.

The Turkomans, veterans of a hundred wild battles, hugged their boulders and kept aiming and firing without the slightest confusion. The men on the plateau were kicking up the devil's own din. They were caught in the jaws of the vise, with bullets coming from both ways, and no way of knowing the exact numbers of their new assailants.

The break came with hurricane suddenness, as is nearly always the case in hill fighting. The men on the plain broke and fled westward, a disorderly mob, scrambling over boulders and leaping gullies, their tattered garments flapping in the wind.

The Turkomans sent a last volley into their backs, toppling over distant figures like tenpins, and the men in the tower gave tongue and began scrambling down into the pass.

O'Donnell cast a practised eye at the fleeing marauders, knew that the rout was final, and called for the ten men below him to bring up the horses swiftly. He had an eye for dramatics, and he knew the effect they would make filing over the ridge and out across the boulder-strewn plain on their Turkish steeds.

A few minutes later he enjoyed that effect and the surprised yells of the men they had aided as they saw the Astrakhan *kalpaks* of the riders top the ridge. The pass was crowded with men in ragged garments, grasping rifles, and in evident doubt as to the status of the newcomers.

O'Donnell headed straight for the ravine, which was nearer the ridge than it was to the pass, believing the Khurukzai chief was among those trapped there.

His rifle was slung on his back, and his open right hand raised as a sign of peace; seeing which the men in

the pass dubiously lowered their rifles and came
streaming across the plateau toward him, instead of
pursuing the vanquished, who were already disappear-
ing among the distant crags and gulches.

A dozen steps from the edge of the ravine O'Donnell
drew rein, glimpsing turbans among the rocks, and
called out a greeting in *Pashtu.* A deep bellowing voice
answered him, and a vast figure heaved up into full
view, followed by half a dozen lesser shapes.

"Allah be with thee!" roared the first man.

He was tall, broad, and powerful; his beard was
stained with henna, and his eyes blazed like fires
burning under gray ice. One massive fist gripped a rifle,
the thumb of the other was hooked into the broad
silken girdle which banded his capacious belly, as he
tilted back on his heels and thrust his beard out
truculently. That girdle likewise supported a broad
tulwar and three or four knives.

"*Mashallah!*" roared this individual. "I had thought
it was my own men who had taken the dogs in the rear,
until I saw those fur caps. Ye are Turks from
Shahrazar, no doubt?"

"Aye; I am Ali el Ghazi, a Kurd, brother-in-arms to
Orkhan Bahadur. You are Ahmed Shah, lord of
Khuruk?"

There was a hyena-like cackle of laughter from the
lean, evil-eyed men who had followed the big man out
of the gully.

"Ahmed Shah has been in hell these four days,"
rumbled the giant. "I am Afzal Khan, whom men name
the Butcher."

O'Donnell sensed rather than heard a slight stir
among the men behind him. Most of them understood
Pashtu, and the deeds of Afzal Khan had found echo in

the *serais* of Turkestan. The man was an outlaw, even in that lawless land, a savage plunderer whose wild road was lurid with the smoke and blood of slaughter.

"But that pass is the gateway to Khuruk," said O'Donnell, slightly bewildered.

"Aye!" agreed Afzal Khan affably. "Four days ago I came down into the valley from the east and drove out the Khurukzai dogs. Ahmed Shah I slew with my own hands—so!"

A flicker of red akin to madness flamed up momentarily in his eyes as he smashed the butt of his rifle down on a dead tamarisk branch, shattering it from the trunk. It was as if the mere mention of murder roused the sleeping devil in him. Then his beard bristled in a fierce grin.

"The villages of Khuruk I burned," he said calmly. "My men need no roofs between them and the sky. The village dogs—such as still lived—fled into the hills. This day I was hunting some from among the rocks, not deeming them wise enough to plant an ambush, when they cut me off from the pass, and the rest you know. I took refuge in the ravine. When I heard your firing I thought it was my own men."

O'Donnell did not at once answer, but sat his horse, gazing inscrutably at the fierce, scarred countenance of the Afghan. A sidelong glance showed him the men from the tower straggling up—some seventy of them, a wild, dissolute band, ragged and hairy, with wolfish countenances and rifles in their hands. These rifles were, in most cases, inferior to those carried by his own men.

In a battle begun then and there, the advantage was still with the mounted Turkomans. Then another glance showed him more men swarming out of the pass—a hundred at least.

"The dogs come at last!" grunted Afzal Khan. "They have been gorging back in the valley. I would have been vulture bait if I had been forced to await their coming. Brother!" He strode forward to lay his hand on O'Donnell's stirrup strap, while envy of the admiration for the magnificent Turkish stallion burned in his fierce eyes. "Brother, come with me to Khuruk! You have saved my life this day, and I would reward you fittingly."

O'Donnell did not look at his Turkomans. He knew they were waiting for his orders and would obey him. He could draw his pistol and shoot Afzal Kahn dead, and they could cut their way back across the plateau in the teeth of the volleys that were sure to rake their line of flight. Many would escape. But why escape? Afzal Khan had every reason to show them the face of a friend, and, besides, if he had killed Ahmed Shah, it was logical to suppose that he had the papers without which O'Donnell dared not return to Shahrazar.

"We will ride with you to Khuruk, Afzal Khan," decided O'Donnell.

The Afghan combed his crimson beard with his fingers and boomed his gratification.

The ragged ruffians closed in about them as they rode toward the pass, a swarm of sheepskin coats and soiled turbans that hemmed in the clean-cut riders in their fur caps and girdled *kaftans*.

O'Donnell did not miss the envy in the glances cast at the rifles and cartridge belts and horses of the Turkomans. Orkhan Bahadur was generous with his men to the point of extravagance; he had sent them out with enough ammunition to fight a small war.

Afzal Khan strode by O'Donnell's stirrup, booming his comments and apparently oblivious to everything except the sound of his own voice.

O'Donnell glanced from him to his followers. Afzal Khan was a Yusufzai, a pure-bred Afghan, but his men were a motley mob—Pathans, mostly, Orakzai, Ummer Khels, Sudozai, Afridis, Ghilzai—outcasts and nameless men from many tribes.

They went through the pass—a knifecut gash between sheer rock walls, forty feet wide and three hundred yards long—and beyond the tower were a score of gaunt horses which Afzal Khan and some of his favored henchmen mounted. Then the chief gave pungent orders to his men; fifty of them climbed into the tower and resumed the ceaseless vigilance that is the price of life in the hills, and the rest followed him and his guests out of the pass and along the knife-edge trail that wound amid savage crags and jutting spurs.

Afzal Khan fell silent, and indeed there was scant opportunity for conversation, each man being occupied in keeping his horse or his own feet on the wavering path. The surrounding crags were so rugged and lofty that the strategic importance of the Pass of Akbar impressed itself still more strongly on O'Donnell.

Only through that pass could any body of men make their way safely. He felt uncomfortably like a man who sees a door shut behind him, blocking his escape, and he glanced furtively at Afzal Khan, riding with stirrups so short that he squatted like a huge toad in his saddle. The chief seemed preoccupied; he gnawed a wisp of his red beard and there was a blank stare in his eyes.

The sun was swinging low when they came to a second pass. This was not exactly a pass at all, in the usual sense. It was an opening in a cluster of rocky spurs that rose like fangs along the lip of a rim beyond which the land fell away in a long gradual sweep. Threading among these stony teeth, O'Donnell looked down into the valley of Khuruk.

It was not a deep valley, but it was flanked by cliffs that looked unscalable. It ran east and west, roughly, and they were entering it at the eastern end. At the western end it seemed to be blocked by a mass of crags.

There were no cultivated patches, or houses to be seen in the valley—only stretches of charred ground. Evidently the destruction of the Khurukzai villages had been thorough. In the midst of the valley stood a square stone inclosure, with a tower at one corner, such as are common in the hills, and serve as forts in times of strife.

Divining his thought, Afzal Khan pointed to this and said: "I struck like a thunderbolt. They had not time to take refuge in the *sangar*. Their watchmen on the heights were careless. We stole upon them and knifed them; then in the dawn we swept down on the villages. Nay, some escaped. We could not slay them all. They will keep coming back to harass me—as they have done this day—until I hunt them down and wipe them all out."

O'Donnell had not mentioned the papers; to have done so would have been foolish; he could think of no way to question Afzal Khan without waking the Afghan's suspicions; he must await his opportunity.

That opportunity came unexpectedly.

"Can you read *Urdu?*" asked Afzal Khan abruptly.

"Aye!" O'Donnell made no further comment but waited with concealed tenseness.

"I cannot; nor *Pashtu,* either, for that matter," rumbled the Afghan. "There were papers on Ahmed Shah's body, which I believe are written in *Urdu.*"

"I might be able to read them for you."

O'Donnell tried to speak casually, but perhaps he was not able to keep his eagerness altogether out of his voice. Afzal Khan tugged his beard, glanced at him sidewise, and changed the subject. He spoke no more of the papers and made no move to show them to his guest. O'Donnell silently cursed his own impatience; but at least he had learned that the documents he sought were in the bandit's possession, and that Afzal Khan was ignorant of their nature—if he was not lying.

At a growled order all but sixty of the chief's men halted among the spurs overlooking the valley. The rest trailed after him.

"They watch for the Khurukzai dogs," he explained. "There are trails by which a few men might get through the hills, avoiding the Pass of Akbar, and reach the head of the valley."

"Is this the only entrance to Khuruk?"

"The only one that horses can travel. There are footpaths leading through the crags from the north and the south, but I have men posted there as well. One rifleman can hold any one of them forever. My forces are scattered about the valley. I am not to be taken by surprise as I took Ahmed Shah."

The sun was sinking behind the western hills as they rode down the valley, tailed by the men on foot. All were strangely silent, as if oppressed by the silence of the plundered valley. Their destination evidently was the inclosure, which stood perhaps a mile from the head of the valley. The valley floor was unusually free of boulders and stones, except a broken ledge like a reef that ran across the valley several hundred yards east of the fortalice. Halfway between these rocks and the inclosure, Afzal Khan halted.

"Camp here!" he said abruptly, with a tone more of command than invitation. "My men and I occupy the *sangar,* and it is well to keep our wolves somewhat apart. There is a place where your horses can be stabled, where there is plenty of fodder stored." He pointed out a stone-walled pen of considerable dimensions a few hundred yards away, near the southern cliffs. "Hungry wolves come down from the gorges and attack the horses."

"We will camp beside the pen," said O'Donnell, preferring to be closer to their mounts.

Afzal Khan showed a flash of irritation. "Do you wish to be shot in the dark for an enemy?" he growled. "Pitch your tents where I bid you. I have told my men at the pass where you will camp, and if any of them come down the valley in the dark, and hear men where no men are supposed to be, they will shoot first and investigate later. Besides, the Khurukzai dogs, if they creep upon the crags and see men sleeping beneath them, will roll down boulders and crush you like insects."

This seemed reasonable enough, and O'Donnell had no wish to antagonize Afzal Khan. The Afghan's attitude seemed a mixture of his natural domineering arrogance and an effort at geniality. This was what might be expected, considering both the man's nature and his present obligation. O'Donnell believed that Afzal Khan begrudged the obligation, but recognized it.

"We have no tents," answered the American. "We need none. We sleep in our cloaks." And he ordered his men to dismount at the spot designated by the chief. They at once unsaddled and led their horses to the pen, where, as the Afghan had declared, there was an abundance of fodder.

O'Donnell told off five men to guard them. Not, he hastened to explain to the frowning chief, that they feared human thieves, but there were the wolves to be considered. Afzal Khan grunted and turned his own sorry steeds into the pen, growling in his beard at the contrast they made alongside the Turkish horses.

His men showed no disposition to fraternize with the Turkomans; they entered the inclosure and presently the smoke of cooking fires arose. O'Donnell's own men set about preparing their scanty meal, and Afzal Khan came and stood over them, combing his crimson beard that the firelight turned to blood. The jeweled hilts of his knives gleamed in the glow, and his eyes burned red like the eyes of a hawk.

"Our fare is poor," he said abruptly. "Those Khurukzai dogs burned their own huts and food stores when they fled before us. We are half starved. I can offer you no food, though you are my guests. But there is a well in the *sangar,* and I have sent some of my men to fetch some steers we have in a pen outside the valley. Tomorrow we shall all feast full, *inshallah!*"

O'Donnell murmured a polite response, but he was conscious of a vague uneasiness. Afzal Khan was acting in a most curious manner, even for a bandit who trampled all laws and customs of conventional conduct. He gave them orders one instant and almost apologized for them in the next.

The matter of designating the camp site sounded almost as if they were prisoners, yet he had made no attempt to disarm them. His men were sullen and silent, even for bandits. But he had no reason to be hostile toward his guests, and, even if he had, why had he brought them to Khuruk, when he could have wiped them out up in the hills just as easily?

"Ali el Ghazi," Afzal Khan suddenly repeated the name. "Wherefore Ghazi? What infidel didst thou slay to earn the name?"

"The Russian, Colonel Ivan Kurovitch." O'Donnell

spoke no lie there. As Ali el Ghazi, a Kurd, he was known as the slayer of Kurovitch; the duel had occurred in one of the myriad nameless skirmishes along the border.

Afzal Khan meditated this matter for a few minutes. The firelight cast part of his features in shadow, making his expression seem even more sinister than usual. He loomed in the firelit shadows like a somber monster weighing the doom of men. Then with a grunt he turned and strode away toward the *sangar*.

III

Night had fallen. Wind moaned among the crags. Cloud masses moved across the dark vault of the night, obscuring the stars, which blinked here and there, were blotted out and then reappearing, like chill points of frosty silver. The Turkomans squatted silently about their tiny fires, casting furtive glances over their shoulders.

Men of the deserts, the brooding grimness of the dark mountains daunted them; the night pressing down in the bowl of the valley dwarfed them in its immensity. They shivered at the wailing of the wind, and peered fearfully into the darkness, where, according to their superstitions, the ghosts of murdered men roamed ghoulishly. They stared bleakly at O'Donnell, in the grip of fear and paralyzing fatalism.

The grimness and desolation of the night had its effect on the American. A foreboding of disaster oppressed him. There was something about Afzal Khan he could not fathom—something unpredictable.

The man had lived too long outside the bounds of ordinary humanity to be judged by the standards of common men. In his present state of mind the bandit chief assumed monstrous proportions, like an ogre out of a fable.

O'Donnell shook himself angrily. Afzal Khan was only a man, who would die if bitten by lead or steel, like any other man. As for treachery, what would be the motive? Yet the foreboding remained.

"Tomorrow we will feast," he told his men. "Afzal Khan has said it."

They stared at him somberly, with the instincts of the black forests and the haunted steppes in their eyes which gleamed wolfishly in the firelight.

"The dead feast not," muttered one of them.

"What talk is this?" rebuked O'Donnell. "We are living men, not dead."

"We have not eaten salt with Afzal Khan," replied the Turkoman. "We camp here in the open, hemmed in by his slayers on either hand. Aie, we are already dead men. We are sheep led to the butcher."

O'Donnell stared hard at his men, startled at their voicing the vague fears that troubled him. There was no accusation of his leadership in their voices. They merely spoke their beliefs in a detached way that belied the fear in their eyes. They believed they were to die, and he was beginning to believe they were right. The fires were dying down, and there was no more fuel to build them up. Some of the men wrapped themselves in their cloaks and lay down on the hard ground. Others remained sitting cross-legged on their saddle cloths, their heads bent on their breasts.

O'Donnell rose and walked toward the first outcropping of the rocks, where he turned and stared back at the inclosure. The fires had died down there to a glow. No sound came from the sullen walls. A mental picture formed itself in his mind, resultant from his visit to the redoubt for water.

It was a bare wall inclosing a square space. At the northwest corner rose a tower. At the southwest corner there was a well. Once a tower had protected the well, but now it was fallen into ruins, so that only a hint of it remained. There was nothing else in the inclosure except a small stone hut with a thatched roof. What was in the hut he had no way of knowing. Afzal Khan had remarked that he slept alone in the tower. The chief did not trust his own men too far.

What was Afzal Khan's game? He was not dealing straight with O'Donnell; that was obvious. Some of his evasions and pretenses were transparent; the man was not as clever as one might suppose; he was more like a bull that wins by ferocious charges.

But why should he practice deception? What had he to gain? O'Donnell had smelled meat cooking in the fortalice. There was food in the valley, then, but for some reason the Afghan had denied it. The Turkomans knew that; to them it logically suggested but one thing—he would not share the salt with men he intended to murder. But again, why?

"*Ohai,* Ali el Ghazi!"

At that hiss out of the darkness, O'Donnell wheeled, his big pistol jumping into his hand, his skin prickling. He strained his eyes, but saw nothing; heard only the muttering of the night wind.

"Who is it?" he demanded guardedly. "Who calls?"

"A friend! Hold your fire!"

O'Donnell saw a more solid shadow detach itself from the rocks and move toward him. With his thumb pressing back the fanged hammer of his pistol, he shoved the muzzle against the man's belly and leaned forward to glare into the hairy face in the dim, uncertain starlight. Even so the darkness was so thick the fellow's features were only a blur.

"Do you not know me?" whispered the man, and by his accent O'Donnell knew him for a Waziri. "I am Yar Muhammad!"

"Yar Muhammad!" Instantly the gun went out of sight and O'Donnell's hand fell on the other's bull-like shoulder. "What do you in this den of thieves?"

The man's teeth glimmered in the tangle of his beard as he grinned. "*Mashallah!* Am I not a thief, El Shirkuh?" he asked, giving O'Donnell the name by which the American, in his rightful person, was known to the Moslems. "Hast thou forgotten the old days? Even now the British would hang me, if they could catch me. But no matter. I was one of those who watch the paths in the hills.

"An hour ago I was relieved, and when I returned to the *sangar* I heard men talking of the Turkomans who camped in the valley outside, and it was said their chief was the Kurd who slew the infidel Kurovitch. So I knew it was El Shirkuh playing with doom again. Art thou mad, sahib? Death spreads his wings above thee and all thy men. Afzal Khan plots that thou seest no other sunrise."

"I was suspicious of him," muttered the American. "In the matter of food—"

"The hut in the inclosure is full of food. Why waste beef and bread on dead men? Food is scarce enough in these hills—and at dawn you die."

"But why? We saved Afzal Khan's life, and there is no feud—"

"The Jhelum will flow backward when Afzal Khan spares a man because of gratitude," muttered Yar Muhammad.

"But for what reason?"

"By Allah, sahib, are you blind? Reason? Are not fifty Turkish steeds reason enough? Are not fifty rifles with cartridges reason enough? In these hills firearms and cartridges are worth their weight in silver, and a man will murder his brother for a matchlock. Afzal Khan is a robber, and he covets what you possess.

"These weapons and these horses would lend him great strength. He is ambitious. He would draw to him many more men, make himself strong enough at last to dispute the rule of these hills with Orkhan Bahadur. Nay, he plots some day to take Shahrazar from the Turkoman as he in his turn took it from the Uzbeks. What is the goal of every bandit in these hills, rich or poor? *Mashallah!* The treasure of Khuwarezm!"

O'Donnell was silent, visualizing that accursed hoard as a monstrous loadstone drawing all the evil passions of men from near lands and far. Now it was but an empty shadow men coveted, but they could not know it, and its evil power was as great as ever. He felt an insane desire to laugh.

The wind moaned in the dark, and Yar Muhammad's muttering voice merged eerily with it, unintelligible a yard away.

"Afzal Khan feels no obligation toward you, because you thought it was Ahmed Shah you were aiding. He did not attack you at the Pass because he knew you would slay many of his men, and he feared lest the horses take harm in the battle. Now he has you in a trap as he planned. Sixty men inside the *sangar;* a hundred more at the head of the valley. A short time before moonrise, the men among the spurs will creep down the valley and take position among these rocks. Then when the moon is well risen, so that a man may aim, they will rake you with rifle fire.

"Most of the Turkomans will die in their sleep, and such as live and seek to flee in the other direction will be shot by the men in the inclosure. These sleep now, but sentries keep watch. I slipped out over the western side and have been lying here wondering how to approach your camp without being shot for a prowler.

"Afzal Khan has plotted well. He has you in the perfect trap, with the horses well out of the range of the bullets that will slay their riders."

"So," murmured O'Donnell. "And what is your plan?"

"Plan? Allah, when did I ever have a plan? Nay, that is for you! I know these hills, and I can shoot straight and strike a good blow." His yard-long Khyber knife thrummed as he swung it through the air. "But I only follow where wiser men lead. I heard the men talk, and I came to warn you, because once you turned an Afridi blade from my breast, and again you broke the lock on the Peshawar jail where I lay moaning for the hills!"

O'Donnell did not express his gratitude; that was not necessary. But he was conscious of a warm glow toward the hairy ruffian. Man's treachery is balanced by man's loyalty, at least in the barbaric hills where civilized sophistry has not crept in with its cult of time-serving.

"Can you guide us through the mountains?" asked O'Donnell.

"Nay, sahib; the horses cannot follow these paths; and these booted Turks would die on foot."

"It is nearly two hours yet until moonrise,"

O'Donnell muttered. "To saddle horses now would be to betray us. Some of us might get away in the darkness, but—"

He was thinking of the papers that were the price of his life; but it was not altogether that. Flight in the darkness would mean scattered forces, even though they cut their way out of the valley. Without his guidance the Turkomans would be hopelessly lost; such as were separated from the main command would perish miserably.

"Come with me," he said at last, and hurried back to the men who lay about the charring embers.

At his whisper they rose like ghouls out of the blackness and clustered about him, muttering like suspicious dogs at the Waziri. O'Donnell could scarcely make out the hawklike faces that pressed close about him. All the stars were hidden by dank clouds. The fortalice was but a shapeless bulk in the darkness, and the flanking mountains were masses of solid blackness. The whining wind drowned voices a few yards away.

"Hearken and speak not," O'Donnell ordered. "This is Yar Muhammad, a friend and a true man. We are betrayed. Afzal Khan is a dog, who will slay us for our horses. Nay, listen! In the *sangar* there is a thatched hut. I am going into the inclosure and fire that thatch. When you see the blaze, and hear my pistol speak, rush the wall. Some of you will die, but the surprise will be on our side. We must take the *sangar* and hold it against the men who will come down the valley at moonrise. It is a desperate plan, but the best that offers itself."

"*Bismillah!*" they murmured softly, and he heard the rasp of blades clearing their scabbards.

"This is work indeed for cold steel," he said. "You

must rush the wall and swarm it while the Pathans are dazed with surprise. Send one man for the warriors at the horse pen. Be of good heart; the rest is on Allah's lap."

As he crept away in the darkness, with Yar Muhammad following him like a bent shadow, O'Donnell was aware that the attitude of the Turkomans had changed; they had wakened out of their fatalistic lethargy into fierce tension.

"If I fall," O'Donnell murmured, "will you guide these men back to Shahrazar? Orkhan Bahadur will reward you."

"Shaitan eat Orkhan Bahadur," answered Yar Muhammad. "What care I for these *Turki* dogs? It is you, not they, for whom I risk my skin."

O'Donnell had given the Waziri his rifle. They swung around the south side of the inclosure, almost crawling on their bellies. No sound came from the breastwork, no light showed. O'Donnell knew that they were invisible to whatever eyes were straining into the darkness along the wall. Circling wide, they approached the unguarded western wall.

"Afzal Khan sleeps in the tower," muttered Yar Muhammad, his lips close to O'Donnell's ear. "Sleeps or pretends to sleep. The men slumber beneath the eastern wall. All the sentries lurk on that side, trying to watch the Turkomans. They have allowed the fires to die, to lull suspicion."

"Over the wall, then," whispered O'Donnell, rising and gripping the coping. He glided over with no more noise than the wind in the dry tamarisk, and Yar Muhammad followed him as silently. He stood in the thicker shadow of the wall, placing everything in his mind before he moved.

The hut was before him, a blob of blackness. It looked eastward and was closer to the west wall than to the other. Near it a cluster of dying coals glowed redly. There was no light in the tower, in the northwest angle of the wall.

Bidding Yar Muhammad remain near the wall, O'Donnell stole toward the embers. When he reached them he could make out the forms of the men sleeping between the hut and the east wall. It was like these hardened killers to sleep at such a time. Why not? At the word of their master they would rise and slay. Until the time came it was good to sleep. O'Donnell himself had slept, and eaten, too, among the corpses of a battlefield.

Dim figures along the wall were sentinels. They did not turn; motionless as statues they leaned on the wall staring into the darkness out of which, in the hills, anything might come.

There was a half-burned faggot dying in the embers, one end a charring stump which glowed redly. O'Donnell reached out and secured it. Yar Muhammad, watching from the wall, shivered, though he knew what it was. It was as if a detached hand had appeared for an instant in the dim glow and then disappeared, and then a red point moved toward him.

"Allah!" swore the Waziri. "This blackness is that of Jehannum!"

"Softly!" O'Donnell whispered at him from the pit darkness. "Be ready; now is the beginning of happenings."

The ember glowed and smoked as he blew cautiously upon it. A tiny tongue of flame grew, licking at the wood.

"Commend thyself to Allah!" said O'Donnell, and whirling the brand in a flaming wheel about his head, he cast it into the thatch of the hut.

There was a tense instant in which a tongue of flame flickered and crackled, and then in one hungry combustion the dry stuff leaped ablaze, and the figures of men started out of blank blackness with startling clarity. The guards wheeled, their stupid astonishment etched in the glare, and men sat up in their cloaks on the ground, gaping bewilderedly.

And O'Donnell yelled like a hungry wolf and began jerking the trigger of his pistol.

A sentinel spun on his heel and crumpled, discharging his rifle wildly in the air. Others were howling and staggering like drunken men, reeling and falling in the lurid glare. Yar Muhammad was blazing away with O'Donnell's rifle, shooting down his former companions as cheerfully as if they were ancient enemies.

A matter of seconds elapsed between the time the blaze sprang up and the time when the men were scurrying about wildly, etched in the merciless light and unable to see the two men who crouched in the shadow of the far wall, raining them with lead. But in that scant instant there came another sound—a swift thudding of feet, the daunting sound of men rushing through the darkness in desperate haste and desperate silence.

Some of the Pathans heard it and turned to glare into the night. The fire behind them rendered the outer darkness more impenetrable. They could not see the death that was racing fleetly toward them, until the charge reached the wall.

Then a yell of terror went up as the men along the wall caught a glimpse of glittering eyes and flickering steel rushing out of the blackness. They fired one wild, ragged volley, and then the Turkomans surged up over the wall in an irresistible wave and were slashing and hacking like madmen among the defenders.

Scarcely wakened, demoralized by the surprise, and by the bullets that cut them down from behind, the Pathans were beaten almost before the fight began. Some of them fled over the wall without any attempt at defense, but some fought, snarling and stabbing like wolves. The blazing thatch etched the scene in a lurid glare. *Kalpaks* mingled with turbans, and steel flickered over the seething mob. Yataghans grated against tulwars, and blood spurted.

His pistol empty, O'Donnell ran toward the tower. He had momentarily expected Afzal Khan to appear. But in such moments it is impossible to retain a proper estimate of time. A minute may seem like an hour, an hour like a minute. In reality, the Afghan chief came storming out of the tower just as the Turkomans came surging over the wall. Perhaps he had really been asleep, or perhaps caution kept him from rushing out sooner. Gunfire might mean rebellion against his authority.

At any rate he came roaring like a wounded bull, a rifle in his hands. O'Donnell rushed toward him, but the Afghan glared beyond him to where his swordsmen were falling like wheat under the blades of the maddened Turkomans. He saw the fight was already lost, as far as the men in the inclosure were concerned, and he sprang for the nearest wall.

O'Donnell raced to pull him down, but Afzal Khan, wheeling, fired from the hip. The American felt a heavy blow in his belly, and then he was down on the ground, with all the breath gone from him. Afzal Khan yelled in triumph, brandished his rifle, and was gone over the wall, heedless of the vengeful bullet Yar Muhammad sped after him.

The Waziri had followed O'Donnell across the inclosure and now he knelt beside him, yammering as he fumbled to find the American's wound.

"Aie!" he bawled. "He is slain! My friend and brother! Where will his like be found again? Slain by the bullet of a hillman! Aie! Aie! Aie!"

"Cease thy bellowing, thou great ox," gasped O'Donnell, sitting up and shaking off the frantic hands. "I am unhurt."

Yar Muhammad yelled with surprise and relief. "But the bullet, brother? He fired at point-blank range!"

"It hit my belt buckle," grunted O'Donnell, feeling the heavy gold buckle, which was bent and dented. "By Allah, the slug drove it into my belly. It was like being hit with a sledge hammer. Where is Afzal Khan?"

"Fled away in the darkness."

O'Donnell rose and turned his attention to the fighting. It was practically over. The remnants of the Pathans were fleeing over the wall, harried by the triumphant Turkomans, who in victory were no more merciful than the average Oriental. The *sangar* looked like a shambles.

The hut still blazed brightly, and O'Donnell knew that the contents had been ignited. What had been an advantage was now a danger, for the men at the head of the valley would be coming at full run, and in the light of the fire they could pick off the Turkomans from the darkness. He ran forward shouting orders, and setting an example of action.

Men began filling vessels—cooking pots, gourds, even *kalpaks* from the well and casting the water on the

fire. O'Donnell burst in the door and began to drag out
the contents of the huts, foods mostly, some of it
brightly ablaze, to be doused.

Working as only men in danger of death can work,
they extinguished the flame and darkness fell again
over the fortress. But over the eastern crags a faint
glow announced the rising of the moon through the
breaking clouds.

Then followed a tense period of waiting, in which
the Turkomans hugged their rifles and crouched along
the wall, staring into the darkness as the Pathans had
done only a short time before. Seven of them had been
killed in the fighting and lay with the wounded beside
the well. The bodies of the slain Pathans had been
unceremoniously heaved over the wall.

The men at the valley head could not have been on
their way down the valley when the fighting broke
out, and they must have hesitated before starting,
uncertain as to what the racket meant. But they were
on their way at last, and Afzal Khan was trying to
establish a contact with them.

The wind brought snatches of shouts down the
valley, and a rattle of shots that hinted at hysteria.
These were followed by a furious bellowing which
indicated that Afzal Khan's demoralized warriors had
nearly shot their chief in the dark. The moon broke
through the clouds and disclosed a straggling mob of
men gesticulating wildly this side of the rocks to the
east.

O'Donnell even made out Afzal Khan's bulk and,
snatching a rifle from a warrior's hand, tried a long
shot. He missed in the uncertain light, but his warriors
poured a blast of lead into the thick of their enemies
which accounted for a man or so and sent the others
leaping for cover. From the reeflike rocks they began

firing at the wall, knocking off chips of stone but otherwise doing no damage.

With his enemies definitely located, O'Donnell felt more at ease. Taking a torch he went to the tower, with Yar Muhammad hanging at his heels like a faithful ghoul. In the tower were heaped odds and ends of plunder—saddles, bridles, garments, blankets, food, weapons—but O'Donnell did not find what he sought, though he tore the place to pieces. Yar Muhammad squatted in the doorway, with his rifle across his knees, and watched him, it never occurring to the Waziri to inquire what his friend was searching for.

At length O'Donnell paused, sweating from the vigor of his efforts—for he had concentrated much exertion in a few minutes—and swore.

"Where *does* the dog keep those papers?"

"The papers he took from Ahmed Shah?" inquired Yar Muhammad. "Those he always carries in his girdle. He cannot read them, but he believes they are valuable. Men say Ahmed Shah had them from a *Feringi* who died."

IV

Dawn was lifting over the valley of Khuruk. The sun that was not yet visible above the rim of the hills turned the white peaks to pulsing fire. But down in the valley there was none who found time to wonder at the changeless miracle of the mountain dawn. The cliffs rang with the flat echoes of rifle shots, and wisps of smoke drifted bluely into the air. Lead spanged on stone and whined venomously off into space, or thudded sickeningly into quivering flesh. Men howled blasphemously and fouled the morning with their frantic curses.

O'Donnell crouched at a loophole, staring at the rocks whence came puffs of white smoke and singing harbingers of death. His rifle barrel was hot to his hand, and a dozen yards from the wall lay a huddle of white-clad figures.

Since the first hint of light the wolves of Afzal Khan had poured lead into the fortalice from the reeflike ledge that broke the valley floor. Three times they had broken cover and charged, only to fall back beneath the merciless fire that raked them. Hopelessly outnumbered, the advantage of weapons and position counted heavily for the Turkomans.

O'Donnell had stationed five of the best marksmen in the tower and the rest held the walls. To reach the inclosure meant charging across several hundred yards of open space, devoid of cover. All the outlaws were still among the rocks east of the *sangar,* where, indeed, the broken ledge offered the only cover within rifle range of the redoubt.

The Pathans had suffered savagely in the charges, and they had had the worst of the long-range exchanges, both their marksmanship and their weapons being inferior to the Turkomans'. But some of their bullets did find their way through the loopholes. A few yards from O'Donnell a *kaftaned* rider lay in a grotesque huddle, his feet turned so the growing light glinted on his silver boot heels, his head a smear of blood and brains.

Another lay sprawled near the charred hut, his ghastly face frozen in a grin of agony as he chewed spasmodically on a bullet. He had been shot in the belly and was taking a long time in dying, but not a whimper escaped his livid lips.

A fellow with a bullet hole in his forearm was making more racket; his curses, as a comrade probed for the slug with a dagger point, would have curdled the blood of a devil.

O'Donnell glanced up at the tower, whence wisps of smoke drifting told him that his five snipers were alert. Their range was greater than that of the men at the wall, and they did more damage proportionately and were better protected. Again and again they had broken up attempts to get at the horses in the stone pen. This pen was nearer the inclosure than it was to the rocks, and crumpled shapes on the ground showed of vain attempts to reach it.

But O'Donnell shook his head. They had salvaged a large quantity of food from the burning hut; there was a well of good water; they had better weapons and more ammunition than the men outside. But a long siege meant annihilation.

One of the men wounded in the night fighting had died. There remained alive forty-one men of the fifty with which he had left Shahrazar. One of these was dying, and half a dozen were wounded—one probably fatally. There were at least a hundred and fifty men outside.

Afzal Khan could not storm the walls yet. But under the constant toll of the bullets, the small force of the defenders would melt away. If any of them lived and escaped, O'Donnell knew it could be only by a swift, bold stroke. But he had no plan at all.

The firing from the valley ceased suddenly, and a

white turban cloth was waved above the rock of a rifle muzzle.

"*Ohai,* Ali el Ghazi!" came a hail in a bull's roar that could only have issued from Afzal Khan.

Yar Muhammad, squatting beside O'Donnell, sneered. "A trick! Keep thy head below the parapet, sahib. Trust Afzal Khan when wolves knock out their own teeth."

"Hold your fire, Ali el Ghazi!" boomed the distant voice. "I would parley with you!"

"Show yourself!" O'Donnell yelled back.

And without hesitation a huge bulk loomed up among the rocks. Whatever his own perfidy, Afzal Khan trusted the honor of the man he thought a Kurd. He lifted his hands to show they were empty.

"Advance, alone!" yelled O'Donnell, straining to make himself heard.

Someone thrust the butt of a rifle into a crevice of the rocks so it stood muzzle upward, with the white cloth blowing out in the morning breeze, and Afzal Khan came striding over the stones with the arrogance of a sultan. Behind him turbans were poked up above the boulders.

O'Donnell halted him within good earshot, and instantly he was covered by a score of rifles. Afzal Khan did not seem to be disturbed by that, or by the blood lust in the dark hawklike faces glaring along the barrels. Then O'Donnell rose into view, and the two leaders faced one another in the full dawn.

O'Donnell expected accusations of treachery—for, after all, he had struck the first blow—but Afzal Khan was too brutally candid for such hypocrisy.

"I have you in a vise, Ali el Ghazi," he announced without preamble. "But for that Waziri dog who

crouches behind you, I would have cut your throat at
moonrise last night. You are all dead men, but siege
work grows tiresome, and I am willing to forego half
my advantage. I am generous. As reward of victory I
demand either your guns or your horses. Your horses I
have already, but you shall have them back, if you
wish. Throw down your weapons and you may ride out
of Khuruk. Or, if you wish, I will keep the horses, and
you may march out on foot with your rifles. What is
your answer?"

O'Donnell spat toward him, with a typically
Kurdish gesture. "Are we fools, to be hoodwinked by a
dog with scarlet whiskers?" he snarled. "When Afzal
Khan keeps his sworn word, the Indus will flow
backward. Shall we ride out, unarmed, for you to cut
us down in the passes, or shall we march forth on foot,
for you to shoot us from ambush in the hills?

"You lie when you say you have our horses. Ten of
your men have died trying to take them for you. You lie
when you say you have us in the vise. It is *you* who are
in the vise! You have neither food nor water; there is no
other well in the valley but this. You have few
cartridges, because most of your ammunition is stored
in the tower, and *we* hold that."

The fury in Afzal Khan's countenance told
O'Donnell that he had scored with that shot.

"If you had us helpless you would not be offering
terms," O'Donnell sneered. "You would be cutting our
throats, instead of trying to gull us into the open."

"Sons of sixty dogs!" swore Afzal Khan, plucking at
his beard. "I will flay you all alive! I will keep you
hemmed here until you die!"

"If we cannot leave the fortress, you cannot enter
it," O'Donnell retorted. "Moreover you have drawn all
your men but a handful from the passes, and the

Khurukzai will steal upon you and cut off your heads. They are waiting, up in the hills."

Afzal Khan's involuntarily wry face told O'Donnell that the Afghan's plight was more desperate than he had hoped.

"It is a deadlock, Afzal Khan," said O'Donnell suddenly.

"There is but one way to break it." He lifted his voice, seeing that the Pathans under the protection of the truce were leaving their coverts and drawing within earshot. "Meet me there in the open space, man to man, and decide the feud between us two, with cold steel. If I win, we ride out of Khuruk unmolested. If you win, my warriors are at your mercy."

"The mercy of a wolf!" muttered Yar Muhammad.

O'Donnell did not reply. It was a desperate chance, but the only one. Afzal Khan hesitated and cast a searching glance at his men; that scowling hairy horde was muttering among itself. The warriors seemed ill-content, and they stared meaningly at their leader.

The inference was plain; they were weary of the fighting at which they were at a disadvantage, and they wished Afzal Khan to accept O'Donnell's challenge. They feared a return of the Khurukzai might catch them in the open with empty cartridge pouches. After all, if their chief lost to the Kurd, they would only lose the loot they had expected to win. Afzal Khan understood this attitude, and his beard bristled to the upsurging of his ready passion.

"Agreed!" he roared, tearing out his tulwar and throwing away the scabbard. He made the bright broad steel thrum about his head. "Come over the wall and die, thou slayer of infidels!"

"Hold your men where they are!" O'Donnell ordered and vaulted the parapet.

At a bellowed order the Pathans had halted, and the wall was lined with *kalpaks* as the Turkomans watched tensely, muzzles turned upward but fingers still crooked on the triggers. Yar Muhammad followed O'Donnell over the wall, but did not advance from it; he crouched against it like a bearded ghoul, fingering his knife.

O'Donnell wasted no time. Scimitar in one hand and *kindhjal* in the other, he ran lightly toward the burly figure advancing to meet him. O'Donnell was slightly above medium height, but Afzal Khan towered half a head above him. The Afghan's bull-like shoulders and muscular bulk contrasted with the rangy figure of the false Kurd; but O'Donnell's sinews were like steel wires. His Arab scimitar, though neither so broad nor so heavy as the tulwar, was fully as long, and the blade was of unbreakable Damascus steel.

The men seemed scarcely within arm's reach when the fight opened with a dazzling crackle and flash of steel. Blow followed blow so swiftly that the men watching, trained to arms since birth, could scarcely follow the strokes. Afzal Khan roared, his eyes blazing, his beard bristling, and wielding the heavy tulwars as one might wield a camel wand, he flailed away in a frenzy.

But always the scimitar flickered before him, turning the furious blows, or the slim figure of the false Kurd avoided death by the slightest margins, with supple twists and swayings. The scimitar bent beneath the weight of the tulwar, but it did not break; like a serpent's tongue it always snapped straight again, and like a serpent's tongue it flickered at Afzal Khan's breast, his throat, his groin, a constant threat of death that reddened the Afghan's eyes with a tinge akin to madness.

Afzal Khan was a famed swordsman, and his sheer brute strength was more than a man's. But O'Donnell's balance and economy of motion was a marvel to witness. He never set a foot wrong or made a false motion; he was always poised, always a threat, even in retreat, beaten backward by the bull-like rushes of the Afghan. Blood trickled down his face where a furious stroke, beating down his blade, had bitten through his silk turban and into the scalp, but the flame in his blue eyes never altered.

Afzal Khan was bleeding, too, O'Donnell's point, barely missing his jugular, had plowed through his beard and along his jaw. Blood dripping from his beard made his aspect more fearsome than ever. He roared and flailed, until it seemed that the fury of his onslaught would overbalance O'Donnell's perfect mastery of himself and his blade.

Few noticed, however, that O'Donnell had been working his way in closer and closer under the sweep of the tulwar. Now he caught a furious swipe near the hilt and the *kindhjal* in his left hand licked in and out. Afzal Khan's bellow caught in a gasp. There was but that fleeting instant of contact, so brief it was like blur of movement, and then O'Donnell, at arm's length again, was slashing and parrying, but now there was a thread of crimson on the narrow *kindhjal* blade, and blood was seeping in a steady stream through Afzal Khan's broad girdle.

There was the pain and desperation of the damned in the Afghan's eyes, in his roaring voice. He began to weave drunkenly, but he attacked more madly than ever, like a man fighting against time.

His strokes ribboned the air with bright steel and thrummed past O'Donnell's ears like a wind of death, until the tulwar rang full against the scimitar's guard with hurricane force and O'Donnell went to his knee under the impact. "Kurdish dog!" It was a gasp of frenzied triumph. Up flashed the tulwar and the watching hordes gave tongue. But again the *kindhjal* licked out like a serpent's tongue—outward and upward.

The stroke was meant for the Afghan's groin, but a shift of his legs at the instant caused the keen blade to plow through his thigh instead, slicing veins and tendons. He lurched sidewise, throwing out his arm to balance himself. And even before men knew whether he would fall or not, O'Donnell was on his feet and slashed with the scimitar at his head.

Afzal Khan fell as a tree falls, blood gushing from his head. Even so, the terrible vitality of the man clung to life and hate. The tulwar fell from his hand, but, catching himself on his knees, he plucked a knife from his girdle; his hand went back for the throw—then the knife slipped from his nerveless fingers and he crumpled to the earth and lay still.

There was silence, broken by a strident yell from the Turkomans. O'Donnell sheathed his scimitar, sprang swiftly to the fallen giant and thrust a hand into his blood-soaked girdle. His fingers closed on what he had hoped to find, and he drew forth an oilskin-bound packet of papers. A low cry of satisfaction escaped his lips.

In the tense excitement of the fight, neither he nor the Turkomans had noticed that the Pathans had drawn nearer and nearer, until they stood in a ragged semicircle only a few yards away. Now, as O'Donnell stood staring at the packet, a hairy ruffian ran at his back, knife lifted.

A frantic yell from Yar Muhammad warned

O'Donnell. There was no time to turn; sensing rather than seeing his assailant, the American ducked deeply and the knife flashed past his ear, the muscular forearm falling on his shoulder with such force that again he was knocked to his knees.

Before the man could strike again Yar Muhammad's yard-long knife was driven into his breast with such fury that the point sprang out between his shoulder blades. Wrenching his blade free as the wretch fell, the Waziri grabbed a handful of O'Donnell's garments and began to drag him toward the wall, yelling like a madman.

It had all happened in a dizzying instant, the charge of the Pathan, Yar Muhammad's leap and retreat. The other Pathans rushed in, howling like wolves, and the Waziri's blade made a fan of steel about him and O'Donnell. Blades were flashing on all sides; O'Donnell was cursing like a madman as he strove to halt Yar Muhammad's headlong progress long enough to get to his feet, which was impossible at the rate he was being yanked along.

All he could see was hairy legs, and all he could hear was a devil's din of yells and clanging knives. He hewed sidewise at the legs and men howled, and then there was a deafening reverberation, and a blast of lead at close range smote the attackers and mowed them down like wheat. The Turkomans had woken up and gone into action.

Yar Muhammad was berserk. With his knife dripping red and his eyes blazing madly he swarmed over the wall and down on the other side, all asprawl, lugging O'Donnell like a sack of grain, and still unaware that his friend was not fatally wounded.

The Pathans were at his heels, not to be halted so easily this time. The Turkomans fired point-blank into their faces, but they came on, snarling, snatching at the rifle barrels poked over the wall, stabbing upward.

Yar Muhammad, heedless of the battle raging along the wall, was crouching over O'Donnell, mouthing, so crazy with blood lust and fighting frenzy that he was hardly aware of what he was doing, tearing at O'Donnell's clothing in his efforts to discover the wound he was convinced his friend had received.

He could hardly be convinced otherwise by O'Donnell's lurid blasphemy, and then he nearly strangled the American in a frantic embrace of relief and joy. O'Donnell threw him off and leaped to the wall, where the situation was getting desperate for the Turkomans. The Pathans, fighting without leadership, were massed in the middle of the east wall, and the men in the tower were pouring a devastating fire into them, but the havoc was being wreaked in the rear of the horde. The men in the tower feared to shoot at the attackers along the wall for fear of hitting their own comrades.

As O'Donnell reached the wall, the Turkoman nearest him thrust his muzzle into a snarling, bearded face and pulled the trigger, blasting the hillman's head into a red ruin. Then before he could fire again a knife licked over the wall and disemboweled him. O'Donnell caught the rifle as it fell, smashed the butt down on the head of a hillman climbing over the parapet, and left him hanging dead across the wall.

It was all confusion and smoke and spurting blood and insanity. No time to look right or left to see if the Turkomans still held the wall on either hand. He had his hands full with the snarling bestial faces which rose like a wave before him. Crouching on the firing step, he drove the blood-clotted butt into these wolfish faces until a rabid-eyed giant grappled him and bore him back and over.

They struck the ground on the inside, and O'Donnell's head hit a fallen gun stock with a stunning crack. In the moment that his brain swam dizzily the Pathan heaved him underneath, yelled stridently and lifted a knife—then the straining body went suddenly limp, and O'Donnell's face was spattered with blood and brains, as Yar Muhammad split the man's head to the teeth with his Khyber knife.

The Waziri pulled the corpse off and O'Donnell staggered up, slightly sick, and presenting a ghastly spectacle with his red-dabbled face, hands, and garments. The firing, which had lulled while the fighting locked along the wall, now began again. The disorganized Pathans were falling back, were slinking away, breaking and fleeing toward the rocks.

The Turkomans had held the wall, but O'Donnell swore sickly as he saw the gaps in their ranks. One lay dead in a huddle of dead Pathans outside the wall, and five more hung motionless across the wall, or were sprawled on the ground inside. With these latter were the corpses of four Pathans, to show how desperate the brief fight had been. The number of the dead outside was appalling.

O'Donnell shook his dizzy head, shuddering slightly at the thought of how close to destruction his band had been; if the hillmen had had a leader, had kept their wits about them enough to have divided forces and attacked in several places at once—but it takes a keen mind to think in the madness of such a battle. It had been blind, bloody, and furious, and the random-cast dice of fate had decided for the smaller horde.

The Pathans had taken to the rocks again and were firing in a half-hearted manner. Sounds of loud argument drifted down the wind. He set about dressing the wounded as best he could, and while he was so employed, the Pathans tried to get at the horses again. But the effort was without enthusiasm, and a fusillade from the tower drove them back.

As quickly as he could, O'Donnell retired to a corner of the wall and investigated the oilskin-wrapped packet he had taken from Afzal Khan. It was a letter, several sheets of high-grade paper covered with a fine scrawl. The writing was Russ, not *Urdu,* and there were English margin notes in a different hand. These notes made clear points suggested in the letter, and O'Donnell's face grew grim as he read.

How the unknown English secret-service man who had added those notes had got possession of the letter there was no way of knowing; but it had been intended for the man called Suleiman Pasha, and it revealed what O'Donnell had suspected—a plot within a plot; a red and sinister conspiracy concealing itself in a guise of international policy.

Suleiman Pasha was not only a foreign spy; he was a traitor to the men he served. And the tentacles of the plot which revolved about him stretched incredibly southward into high places. O'Donnell swore softly as he read there the names of men trusted by the government they pretended to serve. And slowly a realization crystallized—this letter must never reach Suleiman Pasha. Somehow, in some way, he, Kirby O'Donnell, must carry on the work of that unknown Englishman who had died with his task uncompleted. That letter must go southward, to lay bare black treachery spawning under the heedless feet of government. He hastily concealed the packet as the Waziri approached.

Yar Muhammad grinned. He had lost a tooth, and

his black beard was streaked and clotted with blood which did not make him look any less savage.

"The dogs wrangle with one another," he said. "It is always thus; only the hand of Afzal Khan kept them together. Now men who followed him will refuse to follow one of their own number. They fear the Khurukzai. We also have reason to beware of them. They will be waiting in the hills beyond the Pass of Akbar."

O'Donnell realized the truth of this statement. He believed a handful of Pathans yet held the tower in the pass, but there was no reason to suppose they would not desert their post, now that Afzal Khan was dead. Men trooping down out of the hills told him that the footpaths were no longer guarded. At any time Khurukzai scouts might venture back, learn what was going on, and launch an attack in force.

The day wore on, hot, and full of suffering for the wounded in the inclosure. Only a desultory firing came from the rocks, where continual squabbling seemed to be going on. No further attack was made, and presently Yar Muhammad grunted with gratification.

From the movement among the rocks and beyond them, it was evident that the leaderless outlaw band was breaking up. Men slunk away up the valley, singly or in small bands. Others fought over horses, and one group turned and fired a volley at their former companions before they disappeared among the spurs at the head of the valley. Without a chieftain they trusted, demoralized by losses, short of water and food and ammunition, and in fear of reprisals, the outlaw band melted away, and within an hour from the time the first bolted, the valley of Khuruk was empty except for O'Donnell's men.

* * *

To make sure the retreat was real, O'Donnell secured his horse from the pen and, with Yar Muhammad, rode cautiously to the valley head. The spurs were empty. From the tracks the American believed that the bandits had headed southward, preferring to make their way through the pathless hills rather than fight their way through the vengeful Khurukzai who in all probability still lurked among the crags beyond the Pass of Akbar.

He had to consider these men himself and he grinned wryly at the twist of fate which had made enemies of the very men he had sought in friendship. But life ran that way in the hills.

"Go back to the Turkomans," he requested Yar Muhammad. "Bid them saddle their horses. Tie the wounded into the saddles, and load the spare horses with food and skins of water. We have plenty of spare horses now, because of the men who were slain. It is dusk now, and time we are on our way.

"We shall take our chance on the trails in the dark, for now that the hill paths are unguarded, assuredly the Khurukzai will be stealing back, and I expect an attack on the valley by moonrise, at the latest. Let them find it empty. Perhaps we can make our way through the Pass and be gone while they are stealing through the hills to the attack. At least we will make the attempt and leave the rest to Allah."

Yar Muhammad grinned widely—the prospect of any sort of action seemed to gratify him immensely—and reined his horse down the valley, evidencing all the pride that becomes a man who rides a blooded Turkish steed. O'Donnell knew he could leave the preparations for the journey with him and the Turkomans.

The American dismounted, tied his horse and strode through the rocky spurs to the point where the trail wound out of them and along a boulder-littered narrow level between two slopes. Dusk was gathering, but he could see any body of men that tried to come along that trail.

But he was not expecting attack by that route. Not knowing just what had taken place in the valley, the Khurukzai even if the men in the tower had deserted it, would be too suspicious to follow the obvious road. And it was not attack of any sort that was worrying him.

He took the packet of papers from his girdle and stared at it. He was torn by indecision. There were documents that needed desperately to get to the British outposts. It was almost sheer suicide for one man to start through the hills, but two men, with food and water, might make it.

He could take Yar Muhammad, load an extra horse or two with provisions, and slip away southward. Then let Suleiman Pasha do his worst with Orkhan Bahadur. Long before the emissary could learn of his flight, he and the Waziri would be far out of the vengeful Turkoman's reach. But, then, what of the warriors back there in the *sangar,* making ready for their homeward flight, with implicit trust in Ali el Ghazi?

They had followed him blindly, obeyed his every order, demonstrated their courage and faithfulness beyond question. If he deserted them now, they were doomed. They could never make their way back through the hills without him. Such as were not lost to die of starvation would be slaughtered by the vengeful Khurukzai who would not forget their defeat by these dark-skinned riders.

Sweat started out on O'Donnell's skin in the agony of his mental struggle. Not even for the peace of all India could he desert these men who trusted him. He was their leader. His first duty was to them.

But, then, what of that damning letter? It supplied the key to Suleiman Pasha's plot. It told of hell brewing in the Khyber Hills, of revolt seething on the Hindu plains, of a plot which might be nipped in the bud were the British officials to learn of it in time. But if he returned to Shahrazar with the Turkomans, he must give the letter to Suleiman Pasha or be denounced to Orkhan—and that meant torture and death. He was in the fangs of the vise; he must either sacrifice himself, his men, or the helpless people of India.

"*Ohai,* Ali el Ghazi!" It was a soft hiss behind him, from the shadow of a jutting rock. Even as he started about, a pistol muzzle was pressed against his back.

"Nay, do not move. I do not trust you yet."

Twisting his head about, O'Donnell stared into the dark features of Suleiman Pasha.

"You! How in Shaitan's name—"

"No matter. Give me the papers which you hold in your hand. Give them to me, or, by Allah, I will send you to hell, Kurd!"

With the pistol boring into his back, there was nothing else O'Donnell could do, his heart almost bursting with rage.

Suleiman Pasha stepped back and tucked the papers into his girdle. He allowed O'Donnell to turn and face him, but still kept him covered with the pistol.

"After you had departed," he said, "secret word came to me from the North that the papers for which I sent you were more important than I had dreamed. I dared not wait in Shahrazar for your return, lest something go awry. I rode for Khuruk with some Ghilzais who knew the road. Beyond the Pass of Akbar we were ambushed by the very people we sought. They slew my men, but they spared me, for I was known to one of their headmen. They told me they had been driven forth by Afzal Khan, and I guessed what else had occurred. They said there had been fighting beyond the Pass, for they had heard the sound of firing, but they did not know its nature. There are no men in the tower in the Pass, but the Khurukzai fear a trap. They do not know the outlaws have fled from the valley.

"I wished to get word with you as soon as possible, so I volunteered to go spying for them alone, so they showed me the footpaths. I reached the valley head in time to see the last of the Pathans depart, and I have been hiding here awaiting a chance to catch you alone. Listen! The Turkomans are doomed. The Khurukzai mean to kill them all. But I can save you. We shall dress you in the clothing of a dead Pathan, and I shall say you are a servant of mine who has escaped from the Turkomans.

"I shall not return to Shahrazar. I have business in the Khyber region. I can use a man like you. We shall return to the Khurukzai and show them how to attack and destroy the Turkomans. Then they will lend us an escort southward. Will you come with me and serve me, Kurd?"

"No, you damned swine!" In the stress of the moment O'Donnell spat his fury in English. Suleiman Pasha's jaw dropped, in the staggering unexpectedness of English words from a man he thought to be a Kurd. And in the instant his wits were disrupted by the discovery, O'Donnell, nerved to desperate quickness, was at his throat like a striking cobra.

The pistol exploded once and then was wrenched from the numbed fingers. Suleiman Pasha was fighting in frenzied silence, and he was all steel strings and

catlike thews. But O'Donnell's *kindhjal* was out and
ripping murderously into him again and again. They
went to the earth together in the shadow of the big
rock, O'Donnell stabbing in a berserk frenzy; and then
he realized that he was driving his blade into a dead
man.

He shook himself free and rose, staggering like a
drunken man with the red haze of his murder lust. The
oilskin packet was in his left hand, torn from his
enemy's garments during the struggle. Dusk had given
way to blue, star-flecked darkness. To O'Donnell's ears
came the clink of hoofs on stone, the creak of leather.
His warriors were approaching, still hidden by the
towering ledges. He heard a low laugh that identified
Yar Muhammad.

O'Donnell breathed deeply in vast content. Now he
could guide his men back through the passes to
Shahrazar without fear of Orkhan Bahadur, who
would never know his secret. He could persuade the
Turkoman chief that it would be to his advantage to
send this letter on to the British border. He, as Ali el
Ghazi, could remain in Shahrazar safely, to oppose
subtly what other conspirators came plotting to the
forbidden city.

He smiled as he wiped the blood from his *kindhjal*
and sheathed it. There still remained the Khurukzai,
waiting with murderous patience beyond the Pass of
Akbar, but his soul was at rest, and the prospect of
fighting his way back through the mountains troubled
him not at all. He was as confident of the outcome as if
he already sat in the palace at Shahrazar.

The Curse of The Crimson God

CHAPTER I

IN THE ALLEY OF SATAN

It was dark as the Pit in that evil-smelling Afghan alley down which Kirby O'Donnell, in his disguise of a swashbuckling Kurd, was groping, on a quest as blind as the darkness which surrounded him. It was a sharp, pain-edged cry smiting his ears that changed the whole course of events for him. Cries of agony were no uncommon sound in the twisting alleys of *Medina el Harami,* the City of Thieves, and no cautious or timid man would think of interfering in an affair which was none of his business. But O'Donnell was neither cautious nor timid, and something in his wayward Irish soul would not let him pass by a cry for help.

Obeying his instincts, he turned toward a beam of light that lanced the darkness close at hand, and an instant later was peering through a crack in the close-drawn shutters of a window in a thick stone wall. What he saw drove a red throb of rage through his brain, though years of adventuring in the raw lands of the world should have calloused him by this time. But

O'Donnell could never grow callous to inhuman torture.

He was looking into a broad room, hung with velvet tapestries and littered with costly rugs and couches. About one of these couches a group of men clustered—seven brawny Yusufzai bravos, and two more who eluded identification. On that couch another man was stretched out, a Waziri tribesman, naked to the waist. He was a powerful man, but a ruffian as big and muscular as himself gripped each wrist and ankle. Between the four of them they had him spread-eagled on the couch, unable to move, though the muscles stood out in quivering knots on his limbs and shoulders. His eyes gleamed redly, and his broad breast glistened with sweat. There was a good reason. As O'Donnell looked, a supple man in a red silk turban lifted a glowing coal from a smoking brazier with a pair of silver tongs, and poised it over the quivering breast, already scarred from similar torture.

Another man, taller than the one with the red turban, snarled a question O'Donnell could not understand. The Waziri shook his head violently and spat savagely at the questioner. An instant later the red-hot coal dropped full on the hairy breast, wrenching an inhuman bellow from the sufferer. And, in that instant O'Donnell launched his full weight against the shutters.

The Irish-American was not a big man, but he was all steel and whalebone. The shutters splintered inward with a crash, and he hit the floor inside feet-first, scimitar in one hand and kindhjal in the other. The torturers whirled and yelped in astonishment.

They saw him as a masked, mysterious figure, for he was clad in the garments of a Kurd, with a fold of his flowing *kafiyeh* drawn about his face. Over his mask

his eyes blazed like hot coals, paralyzing them. But only for an instant the scene held, frozen, and then melted into ferocious activity.

The man in the red turban snapped a quick word and a hairy giant lunged to meet the oncoming intruder. The Yusufzai held a three-foot Khyber knife low, and as he charged he ripped murderously upward. But the downward-lashing scimitar met the upward plunging wrist. The hand, still gripping the knife, flew from that wrist in a shower of blood, and the long, narrow blade in O'Donnell's left hand sliced through the knifeman's bull throat, choking the grunt of agony.

Over the crumpling corpse the American leaped at Red Turban and his tall companion. He did not fear the use of firearms. Shots ringing out by night in the Alley of Shaitan were sure to be investigated, and none of the inhabitants of the Alley desired official investigation.

He was right. Red Turban drew a knife, the tall man a sabre.

"Cut him down, Jallad!" snarled Red Turban, retreating before the American's impetuous onslaught. "Achmet, help here!"

The man called Jallad, which means Executioner, parried O'Donnell's slash and cut back. O'Donnell avoided the swipe with a shift that would have shamed the leap of a starving panther, and the same movement brought him within reach of Red Turban who was sneaking in with his knife. Red Turban yelped and leaped back, so narrowly avoiding O'Donnell's *kindhjal* that the lean blade slit his silken vest and the skin beneath. He tripped over a stool and fell sprawling, but before O'Donnell could follow up his advantage, Jallad was towering over him, raining blows with his sabre. There was power as well as skill in the tall man's arm, and for an instant O'Donnell was on the defensive.

But as he parried the lightning-like strokes, the American saw that the Yusufzai Red Turban had called Achmet was advancing, gripping an old Tower musket by the barrel. One smash of the heavy, brass-bound butt would crush a man's head like an egg. Red Turban was scrambling to his feet, and in an instant O'Donnell would find himself hemmed in on three sides.

He did not wait to be surrounded. A flashing swipe of his scimitar, barely parried in time, drove Jallad back on his heels, and O'Donnell whirled like a startled cat and sprang at Achmet. The Yusufzai bellowed and lifted the musket, but the blinding swiftness of the attack had caught him off-guard. Before the blow could fall he was down, writhing in his own blood and entrails, his belly ripped wide open.

Jallad yelled savagely and rushed at O'Donnell, but the American did not await the attack.

There was no one between him and the Waziri on the couch. He leaped straight for the four men who still gripped the prisoner. They let go of the man, shouting with alarm, and drew their tulwars. One struck viciously at the Waziri, but the man rolled off the couch, evading the blow. The next instant O'Donnell was between him and them. They began hacking at the American, who retreated before them, snarling at the Waziri: "Get out! Ahead of me! Quick!"

"Dogs!" screamed Red Turban as he and Jallad rushed across the room. "Don't let them escape!"

"Come and taste of death thyself, dog!" O'Donnell laughed wildly, above the clangor of steel. But even in the hot passion of battle he remembered to speak with a Kurdish accent.

The Waziri, weak and staggering from the torture he had undergone, slid back a bolt and threw open a door. It gave upon a small enclosed court.

"Go!" snapped O'Donnell. "Over the wall while I hold them back!"

He turned in the doorway, his blades twin tongues of death-edged steel. The Waziri ran stumblingly across the court and the men in the room flung themselves howling at O'Donnell. But in the narrow door their very numbers hindered them. He laughed and cursed them as he parried and thrust. Red Turban was dancing around behind the milling, swearing mob, calling down all the curses in his vocabulary on the thievish Kurd! Jallad was trying to get a clean swipe at O'Donnell, but his own men were in the way. Then O'Donnell's scimitar licked out and under a flailing tulwar like the tongue of a cobra, and a Yusufzai, feeling chill steel in his vitals, shrieked and fell dying. Jallad, lunging with a full-arm reach, tripped over the writhing figure and fell. Instantly the door was jammed with squirming, cursing figures, and before they could untangle themselves, O'Donnell turned and ran swiftly across the yard toward the wall over which the Waziri had already disappeared.

O'Donnell leaped and caught the coping, swung himself up, and had one glimpse of a black, winding street outside. Then something smashed sickeningly against his head. It was a stool, snatched by Jallad and hurled with vindictive force as O'Donnell was momentarily outlined against the stars. But O'Donnell did not know what had hit him, for with the impact came oblivion. Limply and silently he toppled from the wall into the shadowy street below.

CHAPTER II

PATHS OF SUSPICION

It was the tiny glow of a flashlight in his face that roused O'Donnell from his unconsciousness. He sat up, blinking, and cursed, groping for his sword. Then the light was snapped off and in the ensuing darkness a voice spoke: "Be at ease, Ali el Ghazi. I am your friend."

"Who the devil are you?" demanded O'Donnell. He had found his scimitar lying on the ground near him, and now he stealthily gathered his legs under him for a sudden spring. He was in the street at the foot of the wall from which he had fallen, and the other man was but a dim bulk looming over him in the shadowy starlight.

"Your friend," repeated the other. He spoke with a Persian accent. "One who knows the name you call yourself. Call me Hassan. It is as good a name as another."

O'Donnell rose, scimitar in hand, and the Persian extended something toward him. O'Donnell caught the glint of steel in the starlight, but before he could strike as he intended, he saw that it was his own *kindhjal* Hassan had picked up from the ground and was offering him, hilt first.

"You are as suspicious as a starving wolf, Ali el Ghazi," laughed Hassan. "But save your steel for your enemies."

"Where are they?" demanded O'Donnell, taking the *kindhjal*.

"Gone. Into the mountains. *On the trail of the blood-stained god.*"

O'Donnell started violently. He caught the Persian's *khalat* in an iron grip and glared fiercely into the man's dark eyes, mocking and mysterious in the starlight.

"Damn you, what do you know of the blood-stained god?" His *kindhjal's* sharp point just touched the Persian's skin below his ribs.

"I know this," said Hassan imperturbably. "I know you came to *Medina el Harami* following thieves who stole from you the map of a treasure greater than Akbar's Hoard. I too came seeking something. I was hiding nearby, watching through a hole in the wall, when you burst into the room where the Waziri was being tortured. How did you know it was they who stole your map?"

"I didn't!" muttered O'Donnell. "I heard the man cry out, and turned aside to stop the torture. If I'd known *they* were the men I was hunting—listen, how much *do* you know?"

"This much," said Hassan. "In the mountains not far from this city, but hidden in an almost inaccessible place, there is an ancient heathen temple which the hill-people fear to enter. The region is forbidden to *Ferengi,* but one Englishman, named Pembroke, *did* find the temple, by accident, and entering it, found an idol crusted with red jewels, which he called the Blood-Stained God. He could not bring it away with him, but he made a map, intending to return. He got safely away, but was stabbed by a fanatic in Kabul and died there. But before he died he gave the map to a Kurd named Ali el Ghazi."

"Well?" demanded O'Donnell grimly. The house behind him was dark and still. There was no other sound in the shadowy street except the whisper of the wind and the low murmur of their voices.

"The map was stolen," said Hassan. "By whom, you know."

"I didn't know at the time," growled O'Donnell. "Later I learned the thieves were an Englishman named Hawklin and a disinherited Afghan prince named Jehungir Khan. Some skulking servant spied on Pembroke as he lay dying, and told them. I didn't know either of them by sight, but I managed to trace them to this city. Tonight I learned they were hiding somewhere in the Alley of Shaitan. I was blindly searching for a clue to their hiding place when I stumbled into that brawl."

"You fought them without knowing they were the men you sought!" said Hassan. "The Waziri was one Yar Muhammad, a spy of Yakub Khan, the Jowaki outlaw chief. They recognized him, tricked him into their house and were burning him to make him tell them the secret trails through the mountains known only to Yakub's spies. Then you came, and you know the rest."

"All except what happened when I climbed the wall," said O'Donnell.

"Somebody threw a stool," replied Hassan. "When you fell beyond the wall they paid no more attention to you, either thinking you were dead, or not having recognized you because of your mask. They chased the Waziri, but whether they caught and killed him, or he got away, I don't know. I do know that after a short chase they returned, saddled horses in great haste and set out westward, leaving the dead men where they fell. I came and uncovered your face, then, to see who you were, and recognized you."

"Then the man in the red turban was Jehungir

Khan," muttered O'Donnell. "But where was Hawk-lin?"

"He was disguised as an Afghan—the man they called Jallad, the Executioner, because he has killed so many men."

"I never dreamed Jallad was a *Ferengi*," growled O'Donnell.

"Not all men are what they seem," said Hassan casually. "I happen to know, for instance, that you are no Kurd at all, but an American named Kirby O'Donnell."

Silence held for a brief tick of time, in which life and death poised on a hair trigger.

"And what then?" O'Donnell's voice was soft and deadly as a cobra's hiss.

"Nothing! Like you I want the red god. That's why I followed Hawklin here. But I can't fight his gang alone. Neither can you. But we can join forces. Let us follow those thieves and take the idol away from them!"

"All right," O'Donnell made a quick decision. "But I'll kill you if you try any tricks, Hassan!"

"Trust me!" answered Hassan. "Come. I have horses at the *serai*—better than the steed which brought you into this city of thieves."

The Persian led the way through narrow, twisting streets, overhung with latticed balconies, and along winding, ill-smelling alleys, until he stopped at the lamp-lit door of an enclosed courtyard. At his knock a bearded face appeared at the wicket, and following a few muttered words the gate swung open. Hassan entered confidently, and O'Donnell followed suspiciously. He half expected a trap of some sort; he had many enemies in Afghanistan, and Hassan was a stranger. But the horses were there, and a word from the keeper of the *serai* set sleepy servants to saddling them, and filling capacious saddle-pouches with packets of food. Hassan brought out a pair of high-powered rifles and a couple of well-filled cartridge belts.

A short time later they were riding together out of the west gate, perfunctorily challenged by the sleepy guard. Men came and went at all hours in *Medina el Harami*. (It goes by another name on the maps, but men swear the ancient Moslem name fits it best.)

Hassan the Persian was portly but muscular, with a broad, shrewd face and dark, alert eyes. He handled his rifle expertly, and a scimitar hung from his hip. O'Donnell knew he would fight with cunning and courage when driven to bay. And he also knew just how far he could trust Hassan. The Persian adventurer would play fair just so long as the alliance was to his advantage. But if the occasion rose when he no longer needed O'Donnell's help, he would not hesitate to murder his partner if he could, so as to have the entire treasure for himself. Men of Hassan's type were as ruthless as a king cobra.

Hawklin was a cobra too, but O'Donnell did not shrink from the odds against them—five well-armed and desperate men. Wit and cold recklessness would even the odds when the time came.

Dawn found them riding through rugged defiles, with frowning slopes shouldering on either hand, and presently Hassan drew rein, at a loss. They had been following a well-beaten road, but now the marks of hoofs turned sharply aside and vanished on the bare rocky floor of a wide plateau.

"Here they left the road," said Hassan. "Thus was Hawklin's steed shod. But we cannot trace them over those bare rocks. You studied the map when you had it—how lies our route from here?"

O'Donnell shook his head, exasperated at this unexpected frustration.

"The map's an enigma, and I didn't have it long enough to puzzle it out. The main landmark, which locates an old trail that runs to the temple should be somewhere near this point. But it's indicated on the map as Akbar's Castle. I never heard of such a castle, or the ruins of any such castle—in these parts or anywhere else."

"Look!" exclaimed Hassan, his eyes blazing, as he started up in his stirrups, and pointed toward a great bare crag that jutted against the skyline some miles to the west of them. "That is Akbar's Castle! It is now called the Crag of Eagles, but in old times they called it Akbar's Castle! I have read of it in an old, obscure manuscript! Somehow Pembroke knew that and called it by its old name to baffle meddlers! Come on! Jehungir Khan must have known that too. We're only an hour behind them, and our horses are better than theirs."

O'Donnell took the lead, cudgelling his memory to recall the details of the stolen map. Skirting the base of the crag to the southwest, he took an imaginary line from its summit to three peaks forming a triangle far to the south. Then he and Hassan rode westward in a slanting course. Where their course intersected the imaginary line, they came on the faint traces of an old trail, winding high up into the bare mountains. The map had not lied and O'Donnell's memory had not failed them. The droppings of horses indicated that a party of riders had passed along the dim trail recently. Hassan asserted it was Hawklin's party, and O'Donnell agreed.

"They set their course by Akbar's Castle, just as we

did. We're closing the gap between us. But we don't want to crowd them too close. They outnumber us. It's up to us to stay out of sight until they get the idol. Then we ambush them and take it away from them."

Hassan's eyes gleamed; such strategy was joy to his Oriental nature.

"But we must be wary," he said. "From here on the country is claimed by Yakub Khan, who robs all he catches. Had they known the hidden paths, they might have avoided him. Now they must trust to luck not to fall into his hands. And we must be alert, too! Yakub Khan is no friend of mine, and he hates Kurds!"

CHAPTER III

SWORDS OF THE CRAGS

Mid-afternoon found them still following the dim path that meandered endlessly on—obviously the trace of an ancient, forgotten road.

"If that Waziri got back to Yakub Khan," said Hassan, as they rode toward a narrow gorge that opened in the frowning slopes that rose about them, "the Jowakis will be unusually alert for strangers. Yar Muhammad didn't suspect Hawklin's real identity, though, and didn't learn what he was after. Yakub won't know, either. I believe he knows where the temple is, but he's too superstitious to go near it. Afraid of ghosts. He doesn't know about the idol. Pembroke was the only man who'd entered that temple in Allah only knows how many centuries. I heard the story from his servant in Peshawur who was dying from a snake bite. Hawklin, Jehungir Khan, you and I are the only men alive who know about the god—"

They reined up suddenly as a lean, hawk-faced Pathan rode out of the gorge mouth ahead of them.

"Halt!" he called imperiously, riding toward them with an empty hand lifted. "By what authority do you ride in the territory of Yakub Khan?"

"Careful," muttered O'Donnell. "He's a Jowaki. There may be a dozen rifles trained on us from those rocks right now."

"I'll give him money," answered Hassan under his breath. "Yakub Khan claims the right to collect toll from all who travel through his country. Maybe that's all this fellow wants."

To the tribesmen he said, fumbling in his girdle; "We are but poor travellers, who are glad to pay the toll justly demanded by your brave chief. We ride alone."

"Then who is that behind you?" harshly demanded the Jowaki, nodding his head in the direction from which they had come. Hassan, for all his wariness, half turned his head, his hand still outstretched with the coins. And in that instant fierce triumph flamed in the dark face of the Jowaki, and in one motion quick as the lunge of a cobra, he whipped a dagger from his girdle and struck at the unsuspecting Persian.

But quick as he was, O'Donnell was quicker, sensing the trap laid for them. As the dagger darted at Hassan's throat, O'Donnell's scimitar flashed in the sun and steel rang loud on steel. The dagger flew from the Pathan's hand, and with a snarl he caught at the rifle butt which jutted from his saddle-scabbard. Before he could drag the gun free, O'Donnell struck again, cleaving the turban and the skull beneath. The

Jowaki's horse neighed and reared, throwing the corpse headlong, and O'Donnell wrenched his own steed around.

"Ride for the gorge!" he yelled. "It's an ambush!"

The brief fight had occupied a mere matter of moments. Even as the Jowaki tumbled to the earth, rifle shots ripped out from the boulders on the slopes. Hassan's horse leaped convulsively and bolted for the mouth of the defile, spattering blood at each stride. O'Donnell felt flying lead tug at his sleeve as he struck in the spurs and fled after the fleeing Persian who was unable to regain control of his pain-maddened beast.

As they swept toward the mouth of the gorge, three horsemen rode out to meet them, proven swordsmen of the Jowaki clan, swinging their broad-bladed tulwars. Hassan's crazed mount was carrying him full into their teeth, and the Persian fought in vain to check him. Suddenly abandoning the effort he dragged his rifle from its boot and started firing point-blank as he came on. One of the oncoming horses stumbled and fell, throwing its rider. Another rider threw up his arms and toppled earthward. The third man hacked savagely at Hassan as the maddened horse raced past, but the Persian ducked beneath the sweeping blade and fled on into the gorge.

The next instant O'Donnell was even with the remaining swordsman, who spurred at him, swinging the heavy tulwar. The American threw up his scimitar and the blades met with a deafening crash as the horses came together breast to breast. The tribesman's horse reeled to the impact, and O'Donnell rose in his stirrups and smiting downward with all his strength, beat down the lifted tulwar and split the skull of the wielder. An instant later the American was galloping on into the gorge. He half expected it to be full of armed warriors, but there was no other choice. Outside bullets were raining after him, splashing on rocks and ripping into stunted trees.

But evidently the man who set the trap had considered the marksmen hidden among the rocks on the slopes sufficient, and had posted only those four warriors in the gorge, for, as O'Donnell swept into it he saw only Hassan ahead of him. A few yards on the wounded horse stumbled and went down, and the Persian leaped clear as it fell.

"Get up behind me!" snapped O'Donnell, pulling up, and Hassan, rifle in hand, leaped up behind the saddle. A touch of the spurs and the heavily burdened horse set off down the gorge. Savage yells behind them indicated that the tribesmen outside were scampering to their horses, doubtless hidden behind the first ridge. They made a turn in the gorge and the noises became muffled. But they knew the wild hillmen would quickly be sweeping down the ravine after them, like wolves on the death-trail.

"That Waziri spy must have got back to Yakub Khan," panted Hassan. "They want blood, not gold. Do you suppose they've wiped out Hawklin?"

"Hawklin might have passed down this gorge before the Jowakis came up to set their ambush," answered O'Donnell. "Or the Jowakis might have been following him when they sighted us coming and set that trap for us. I've got an idea Hawklin is somewhere ahead of us."

"No matter," answered Hassan. "This horse won't carry us far. He's tiring fast. Their horses may be fresh. We'd better look for a place where we can turn and fight. If we can hold them off until dark maybe we can sneak away."

They had covered perhaps another mile and already they heard faint sounds of pursuit, far behind them, when abruptly they came out into a broad bowl-like place, walled by sheer cliffs. From the midst of this bowl a gradual slope led up to a bottle-neck pass on the other side, the exit to this natural arena. Something unnatural about that bottle-neck struck O'Donnell, even as Hassan yelled and jumped down from the horse. A low stone wall closed the narrow gut of the pass. A rifle cracked from that wall just as O'Donnell's horse threw up its head in alarm at the glint of the sun on the blue barrel. The bullet meant for the rider smashed into the horse's head instead.

The beast lurched to a thundering fall, and O'Donnell jumped clear and rolled behind a cluster of rocks, where Hassan had already taken cover. Flashes of fire spat from the wall, and bullets whined off the boulders about them. They looked at each other with grim, sardonic humour.

"Well, we've found Hawklin!" said Hassan.

"And in a few minutes Yakub Khan will come up behind us and we'll be between the devil and the deep blue sea!" O'Donnell laughed slightly, but their situation was desperate. With enemies blocking the way ahead of them and other enemies coming up the gorge behind them, they were trapped.

The boulders behind which they were crouching protected them from the fire from the wall, but would afford no protection from the Jowakis when they rode out of the gorge. If they changed their position they would be riddled by the men in front of them. If they did not change it, they would be shot down by the Jowakis behind them.

A voice shouted tauntingly: "Come out and get shot, you bloody bounder." Hawklin was making no attempt to keep up the masquerade. "I know you,

Hassan! Who's that Kurd with you? I thought I brained him last night!"

"Yes, a Kurd!" answered O'Donnell. "One called Ali el Ghazi!"

After a moment of astounded silence, Hawklin shouted: "I might have guessed it, you Yankee swine! Oh, I know who you are, all right! Well, it doesn't matter now! We've got you where you can't wriggle!"

"You're in the same fix, Hawklin!" yelled O'Donnell. "You heard the shooting back down the gorge?"

"Sure. Who's chasing you?"

"Yakub Khan and a hundred Jowakis!" O'Donnell purposely exaggerated. "When he's wiped us out, do you think he'll let you get away? After you tried to torture his secrets out of one of his men?"

"You'd better let us join you," advised Hassan, recognizing, like O'Donnell, their one, desperate chance. "There's a big fight coming and you'll need all the help you can get if you expect to get out alive!"

Hawklin's turbaned head appeared over the wall; he evidently trusted the honour of the men he hated, and did not fear a treacherous shot.

"Is that the truth?" he yelled.

"Don't you hear the horses?" O'Donnell retorted.

No need to ask. The gorge reverberated with the thunder of hoofs and with wild yells. Hawklin paled. He knew what mercy he could expect from Yakub Khan. And he knew the fighting ability of the two adventurers—knew how heavily their aid would count in a fight to the death.

"Get in, quick!" he shouted. "If we're still alive when the fight's over we'll decide who gets the idol then!"

Truly it was no time to think of treasure, even of the Crimson God! Life itself was at stake. O'Donnell and

Hassan leaped up, rifles in hand, and sprinted up the slope toward the wall. Just as they reached it the first horsemen burst out of the gorge and began firing. Crouching behind the wall, Hawklin and his men returned the fire. Half a dozen saddles were emptied and the Jowakis, demoralized by the unexpectedness of the volley, wheeled and fled back into the gorge.

O'Donnell glanced at the men Fate had made his allies—the thieves who had stolen his treasure-map and would gladly have killed him fifteen minutes before; Hawklin, grim and hard-eyed in his Afghan guise, Jehungir Khan, dapper even after leagues of riding, and three hairy Yusufzai swashbucklers; addressed variously as Akbar, Suliman and Yusuf. These bared their teeth at him. This was an alliance of wolves, which would last only so long as the common menace lasted.

The men behind the wall began sniping at white-clad figures flitting among the rocks and bushes near the mouth of the gorge. The Jowakis had dismounted and were crawling into the bowl, taking advantage of every bit of cover. Their rifles cracked from behind every boulder and stunted tamarisk.

"They must have been following us," snarled Hawklin, squinting along his rifle barrel. "O'Donnell, you lied! There can't be a hundred men out there."

"Enough to cut our throats, anyway," retorted O'Donnell, pressing his trigger. A man darting toward a rock yelped and crumpled, and a yell of rage went up from the lurking warriors. "Anyway, there's nothing to keep Yakub Khan from sending for reinforcements. His village isn't many hours' ride from here."

Their conversation was punctuated by the steady cracking of the rifle. The Jowakis, well hidden, were suffering little from the exchange.

"We've a sporting chance behind this wall," growled
Hawklin. "No telling how many centuries it's stood
here. I believe it was built by the same race that built
the Red God's temple. You'll find ruins like this all
through these hills. Damn!" He yelled at his men:
"Hold your fire! Our ammunitions's getting low.
They're working in close for a rush. Save your
cartridges for it. We'll mow 'em down when they get
into the open." An instant later he shouted: "Here they
come!"

The Jowakis were advancing on foot, flitting from
rock to rock, from bush to stunted bush, firing as they
came. The defenders grimly held their fire, crouching
low and peering through the shallow crenelations.
Lead flattened against the stone, knocking off chips
and dust. Suliman swore luridly as a slug ripped into
his shoulder. Back in the gorge-mouth O'Donnell
glimpsed Yakub Khan's red beard, but the chief took
cover before he could draw a bead. Wary as a fox,
Yakub was not leading the charge in person.

But his clansmen fought with untamed ferocity.
Perhaps the silence of the defenders fooled them into
thinking their ammunition was exhausted. Perhaps the
blood-lust that burned in their veins overcame their
cunning. At any rate they broke cover suddenly, thirty-
five or forty of them, and rushed up the slope with the
rising ululation of a wolf-pack. Point-blank they fired
their rifles and then lunged at the barrier with three-
foot knives in their hands.

"Now!" screamed Hawklin, and a close-range volley
raked the oncoming horde. In an instant the slope was
littered with writhing figures. The men behind that wall
were veteran fighters, to a man, who could not miss at
that range. The toll taken by their sweeping hail of lead
was appalling but the survivors came on, eyes glaring,

foam on their beards, blades glittering in hairy fists.

"Bullets won't stop 'em!" yelled Hawklin, livid, as he fired his last rifle cartridge. "Hold the wall or we're all dead men!"

The defenders emptied their guns into the thick of the mass and then rose up behind the wall, drawing steel or clubbing rifles. Hawklin's strategy had failed, and now it was hand-to-hand, touch and go, and the devil take the unlucky.

Men stumbled and went down beneath the slash of the last bullets, but over their writhing bodies the horde rolled against the wall and locked there. All up and down the barrier sounded the smash of bone-splintering blows, the rasp and slither of steel meeting steel, the gasping oaths of dying men. The handful of defenders still had the advantage of position, and dead men lay thick at the foot of the wall before the Jowakis got a foothold on the barricade. A wild-eyed tribesman jammed the muzzle of an ancient musket full in Akbar's face, and the discharge all but blew off the Yusufzai's head. Into the gap left by the falling body the howling Jowaki lunged, hurling himself up and over the wall before O'Donnell could reach the spot. The American had stepped back, fumbling to reload his rifle, only to find his belt empty. Just then he saw the raving Jowaki come over the wall. He ran at the man, clubbing his rifle, just as the Pathan dropped his empty musket and drew a long knife. Even as it cleared the scabbard O'Donnell's rifle butt crushed his skull.

O'Donnell sprang over the falling corpse to meet the men swarming on to the wall. Swinging his rifle like a flail, he had no time to see how the fight was going on either side of him. Hawklin was swearing in English, Hassan in Persian, and somebody was screaming in mortal agony. He heard the sound of blows, gasps, curses, but he could not spare a glance to right or left. Three blood-mad tribesmen were fighting like wildcats for a foothold on the wall. He beat at them until his rifle stock was a splintered fragment, and two of them were down with broken heads, but the other, straddling the wall, grabbed the American with gorilla-like hands and dragged him into quarters too close to use his bludgeon. Half throttled by those hairy fingers, on his throat, O'Donnell dragged out his *kindhjal* and stabbed blindly, again and again, until blood gushed over his hand, and with a moaning cry the Jowaki released him and toppled from the wall.

Gasping for air, O'Donnell looked about him, realizing the pressure had slackened. No longer was the barrier massed with wild faces. The Jowakis were staggering down the slope—the few left to flee. Their losses had been terrible, and not a man of those who retreated but streamed blood from some wound.

But the victory had been costly. Suliman lay limply across the wall, his head smashed like an egg. Akbar was dead. Yusuf was dying, with a stab-wound in the belly, and his screams were terrible. As O'Donnell looked he saw Hawklin ruthlessly end his agony with a pistol bullet through the head. Then the American saw Jehungir Khan, sitting with his back against the wall, his hands pressed to his body, while blood seeped steadily between his fingers. The prince's lips were blue, but he achieved a ghastly smile.

"Born in a palace," he whispered. "And I'm dying behind a rock wall! No matter—it is *Kismet*. There is a curse on heathen treasure—men have always died when they rode the trail of the Blood-Stained God—" And he died as he spoke.

Hawklin, O'Donnell and Hassan glanced silently at each other. They were the only survivors—three grim figures, blackened with powder-smoke splashed with blood, their garments tattered. The fleeing Jowakis had vanished in the gorge, leaving the canyon-bowl empty except for the dead men on the slope.

"Yakub got away!" Hawklin snarled. "I saw him sneaking off when they broke. He'll make for his village—get the whole tribe on our trail! Come on! We can find the temple. Let's make a race of it—take the chance of getting the idol and then making our way out of the mountains somehow, before he catches us. We're in this jam together. We might as well forget what's passed and join forces for good. There's enough treasure for the three of us."

"There's truth in what you say," growled O'Donnell. "But you hand over that map before we start."

Hawklin still held a smoking pistol in his hand, but before he could lift it Hassan covered him with a revolver.

"I saved a few cartridges for this," said the Persian, and Hawklin saw the blue noses of the bullets in the chambers. "Give me that gun. Now give the map to O'Donnell."

Hawklin shrugged his shoulders and produced the crumpled parchment. "Damn you, I cut a third of that treasure, if we get it!" he snarled.

O'Donnell glanced at it and thrust it into his girdle.

"All right. I don't hold grudges. You're a swine, but if you play square with us, we'll treat you as an equal partner, eh, Hassan?"

The Persian nodded, thrusting both guns into his girdle. "This is no time to quibble. It will take the best efforts of all three of us if we get out of this alive. Hawklin, if the Jowakis catch up with us I'll give you your pistol. If they don't you won't need it."

CHAPTER IV

TOLL OF THE GOD

There were horses tied in the narrow pass behind the wall. The three men mounted the best beasts, turned the others loose and rode up the canyon that wound away and away beyond the pass. Night fell as they travelled, but through the darkness they pushed recklessly on. Somewhere behind them, how far or how near they could not know, rode the tribesmen of Yakub Khan, and if the chief caught them his vengeance would be ghastly. So through the blackness of the nighted Himalayas they rode, three desperate men on a mad quest, with death on their trail, unknown perils ahead of them, and suspicion of each other edging their nerves.

O'Donnell watched Hassan like a hawk. Search of the bodies at the wall had failed to reveal a single unfired cartridge, so Hassan's pistols were the only firearms left in the party. That gave the Persian an advantage O'Donnell did not relish. If the time came when Hassan no longer needed the aid of his companions, O'Donnell believed the Persian would not scruple to shoot them both down in cold blood. But he would not turn on them as long as he needed their assistance, and when it came to a fight—O'Donnell grimly fingered his blades. More than once he had matched them against hot lead, and lived.

As they groped their way by the starlight, guided by the map which indicated landmarks unmistakable, even by night, O'Donnell found himself wondering

again what it was that the maker of that map had tried
to tell him, just before he died. Death had come to
Pembroke quicker than he had expected. In the very
midst of a description of the temple, blood had gushed
to his lips and he had sunk back, desperately fighting to
gasp a few more words even as he died. It sounded like
a warning—but of what?

Dawn was breaking as they came out of narrow
gorge into a deep, high-walled valley. The defile
through which they entered, a narrow alley between
towering cliffs, was the only entrance; without the map
they would never have found it. It came out upon a
ledge which ran along the valley wall, a jutting shelf a
hundred feet wide with the cliff rising three hundred
feet above it on one hand, and falling away to a
thousand foot drop on the other. There seemed no way
down into the mist-veiled depths of the valley, far
below. But they wasted few glances on what lay below
them, for what they saw ahead of them drove hunger
and fatigue from their minds. There on the ledge stood
the temple, gleaming in the rising sun. It was carved out
of the sheer rock of the cliff, its great portico facing
them. The ledge was like a pathway to its dully-glinting
door.

What race, what culture it represented, O'Donnell
did not try to guess. A thousand unknown conquerors
had swept over these hills before the grey dawn of
history. Nameless civilizations had risen and crumbled
before the peaks shook to the trumpets of Alexander.

"How will we open the door?" O'Donnell wondered.
The great bronze portal looked as though it were built
to withstand artillery. He unfolded the map and
glanced again at the notes scrawled on the margins. But
Hassan slipped from his saddle and ran ahead of them,
crying out in his greed. A strange frenzy akin to

madness had seized the Persian at the sight of the temple, and the thought of the fabulous wealth that lay within.

"He's a fool!" grunted Hawklin, swinging down from his horse. "Pembroke left a warning scribbled on the margin of that map—'The temple can be entered, but be careful, for the god will take his toll.'"

Hassan was tugging and pulling at various ornaments and projections on the portal. They heard him cry out exultantly as it moved under his hands—then his cry changed to a scream of terror as the door, a ton of carved bronze, swayed outward and fell crashing. The Persian had no time to avoid it. It crushed him like an ant. He was completely hidden under the great metal slab from beneath which oozed streams of crimson.

Hawklin shrugged his shoulders.

"I said he was a fool. The ancients knew how to guard their treasure. I wonder how Pembroke escaped being smashed."

"He evidently stumbled on some way to swing the door open without releasing it from its hinges," answered O'Donnell. "That's what happened when Hassan jerked on those knobs. That must have been what Pembroke was trying to tell me when he died— which knobs to pull and which to let alone."

"Well, the god has his toll, and the way's clear for us," grunted Hawklin, callously striding past the encrimsoned door. O'Donnell was close on his heels. Both men paused on the broad threshold, peering into the shadowy interior much as they might have peered into the lair of a serpent. But no sudden doom descended on them, no shape of menace rose before them. They entered cautiously. Silence held the ancient temple, broken only by the soft scuff of their boots.

They blinked in the semi-gloom; out of it a blaze of crimson like a lurid glow of sunset smote their eyes. They saw the blood-stained god, a thing of brass, crusted with flaming gems. It was in the shape of a dwarfish man, and it stood upright on its great splay feet on a block of basalt, facing the door. To the left of it, a few feet from the base of the pedestal, the floor of the temple was cleft from wall to wall by a chasm some fifteen feet wide. At some time or other an earthquake had split the rock, and there was no telling how far it descended into echoing depths. Into that black abyss, ages ago, doubtless screaming victims had been hurled by hideous priests as human sacrifices to the Crimson God. The walls of the temple were lofty and fantastically carved, the roof dim and shadowy above them.

But the attention of the men was fixed avidly on the idol. It was brutish, repellent, a leprous monstrosity, whose red jewels gave it a repellently blood-splashed appearance. But it represented a wealth that made their brains swim.

"God!" breathed O'Donnell. "Those gems are real! They're worth a fortune!"

"Millions!" panted Hawklin. "Too much to share with a damned Yankee!"

It was those words, breathed unconsciously between the Englishman's clenched teeth, which saved O'Donnell's life, dazzled as he was by the blaze of that unholy idol. He wheeled, caught the glint of Hawklin's sabre, and ducked just in time. The whistling blade sliced a fold from his head-dress. Cursing his carelessness—for he might have expected treachery—he leaped back, whipping out his scimitar.

The tall Englishman came in a rush, and O'Donnell

met him, close-pent rage loosing itself in a gust of passion. Back and forth they fought, up and down before the leering idol, feet scuffing swiftly on the rock, blades rasping, slithering and ringing, blue sparks showering as they moved through patches of shadow.

Hawklin was taller than O'Donnell, longer of arm, but O'Donnell was equally strong, and a blinding shade quicker on his feet. Hawklin feared the naked *kindhjal* in his left hand more than he did the scimitar, and he endeavored to keep the fighting at long range, where his superior reach would count heavily. He gripped a dagger in his own left hand, but he knew he could not compete with O'Donnell in knife-play.

But he was full of deadly tricks with the longer steel. Again and again O'Donnell dodged death by the thickness of a hair, and so far his own skill and speed had not availed to break through the Englishman's superb guard.

O'Donnell sought in vain to work into close quarters. Once Hawklin tried to rush him over the lip of the chasm, but nearly impaled himself on the American's scimitar and abandoned the attempt.

Then suddenly, unexpectedly, the end came. O'Donnell's foot slipped slightly on the smooth floor, and his blade wavered for an instant. Hawklin threw all his strength and speed behind a lunging thrust that would have driven his saber clear through O'Donnell's body had it reached its mark. But the American was not as much off-balance as Hawklin thought. A twist of his supple body, and the long lean blade passed beneath his right arm-pit, ploughing through the loose *khalat* as it grazed his ribs. For an instant the blade was caught in the folds of the loose cloth, and Hawklin yelled wildly and stabbed with his dagger. It sank deep in O'Donnell's right arm as he lifted it, and simultaneously the *kindhjal* in O'Donnell's left hand plunged between Hawklin's ribs.

The Englishman's scream broke in a ghastly gurgle. He reeled back, and as O'Donnell tore out the blade, blood spurted and Hawklin fell limply, dead before he hit the floor.

O'Donnell dropped his weapon and knelt, ripping a strip of cloth from his *khalat* for a bandage. His wounded arm was bleeding freely, but a quick investigation assured him that the dagger had not severed any important muscle or vein.

As he bound it up, tying knots with his fingers and teeth, he glanced at the Blood-Stained God which leered down on him and the man he had just slain. It had taken full toll, and it seemed to gloat, with its carven, gargoyle face. He shivered. Surely it must be accursed. Could wealth gained from such a source, and at such a price as the dead man at his feet, ever bring luck? He put the thought from him. The Red God was his, bought by sweat and blood and sword-strokes. He must pack it on a horse and be gone before the vengeance of Yakub Khan overtook him. He could not go back the way he had come. The Jowakis barred that way. He must strike out blindly, through unfamiliar mountains, trusting to luck to make his way to safety.

"Put up your hands!" It was a triumphant shout that rang to the roof.

In one motion he was on his feet, facing the door—then he froze.

Two men stood before him, and one covered him with a cocked rifle. The man was tall, lean and red-bearded.

"Yakub Khan!" ejaculated O'Donnell.

The other man was a powerful fellow who seemed vaguely familiar.

"Drop your weapons!" The chief laughed harshly. "You thought I had run away to my village, did you not? Fool! I sent all my men but one, who was the only one not wounded, to rouse the tribe, while with this man I followed you. I have hung on your trail all night, and I stole in here while you fought with that one on the floor there. Your time has come, you Kurdish dog! Back! Back! Back!"

Under the threat of the rifle O'Donnell moved slowly backward until he stood close to the black chasm. Yakub followed him at a distance of a few feet, the rifle muzzle never wavering.

"You have led me to treasure," muttered Yakub, squinting down the blue barrel in the dim light. "I did not know this temple held such an idol! Had I known, I would have looted it long ago, in spite of the superstition of my followers. Yar Muhammad, pick up his sword and dagger."

At the name the identity of Yakub's powerful follower became clear. The man stooped and picked up the sword, then exclaimed: "Allah!"

He was staring at the brazen hawk's head that formed the pommel of O'Donnell's scimitar.

"Wait!" the Waziri cried. "This is the sword of him who saved me from torture, at the risk of his own life! His face was covered, but I remember the hawk-head on his hilt! This is that Kurd!"

"Be silent!" snarled the chief. "He is a thief and he dies!"

"Nay!" The Waziri was galvanized with the swift, passionate loyalty of the hillman. "He saved my life! Mine, a stranger! What have you ever given me but hard tasks and scanty pay? I renounce my allegiance, you Jowaki thief!"

"Dog!" roared the chief, whirling on Yar Muhammad, who sprang back, being without a gun. Yakub Khan fired from the hip and the bullet sheared a tuft from the Waziri's beard. Yar Muhammad yelled a curse and ran behind the idol's pedestal.

At the crack of the shot O'Donnell was leaping to grapple with the chief, but even as he sprang he saw he would fail. With a snarl Yakub turned the rifle on him, and that fleeting instant O'Donnell knew death would spit from that muzzle before he could reach the Jowaki. Yakub's finger hooked the trigger—and then Yar Muhammad hurled the idol. His mighty muscles creaked as he threw it.

Full against the Jowaki it crashed, bearing him backward—over the lip of the chasm! He fired wildly as he fell, and O'Donnell felt the wind of the bullet. One frenzied shriek rang to the roof as idol and man vanished together.

Stunned, O'Donnell sprang forward and gazed down into the black depths. He looked and listened long, but no sound of their fall ever welled up to him. He shuddered at the realization of that awful depth, and drew back quickly. A hard hand on his shoulder brought him around to look into the grinning, bearded countenance of Yar Muhammad.

"Thou art my comrade henceforth," said the Waziri. "If thou art he who calls himself Ali el Ghazi, is it true that a *Ferengi* lurks beneath those garments?"

O'Donnell nodded, watching the man narrowly.

Yar Muhammad but grinned the more widely.

"No matter! I have slain the chief I followed, and the hands of his tribe will be lifted against me. I must follow another chief—and I have heard many tales of the deeds of Ali el Ghazi! Wilt thou accept me as thy follower, *sahib?*"

"Thou art a man after mine own heart," said O'Donnell, extending his hand, white man fashion.

"Allah favour thee!" Yar Muhammad exclaimed joyously, returning the strong grip. "And now let us go swiftly! The Jowakis will be here before many hours have passed, and they must not find us here! But there is a secret path beyond this temple which leads down into the valley, and I know hidden trails that will take us out of the valley and far beyond their reach before they can get here. Come!"

O'Donnell took up his weapons and followed the Waziri out of the temple. The idol was gone forever, but it had been the price of his life. And there were other lost treasures that challenged a restless adventurer. Already his mind was flying ahead to the search of hidden, golden hoards celebrated in a hundred other legends.

"*Alhamdolillah!*" he said, and laughed with the sheer joy of living as he followed the Waziri to the place where they had left the tethered horses.

The Brazen Peacock

The grisly and fantastic adventure began suddenly enough. I was sitting writing quietly in my room when the door burst open and my Arab servant Ali rushed in, breathless, eyes starting from his head. Close at his heels came a man I thought long dead.

"Girtmann!" I was on my feet in amazement. "What in heaven's name—"

With a motion for silence he turned and, looking carefully out the door, closed and locked it with a sigh of relief. For a moment he breathed heavily as if winded and I looked him over curiously. The years had not changed him—his short, broad figure still evinced dynamic physical power and the strongly carved face with its jutting jaw and hooked nose and arrogant eyes still reflected the stubborn determination and ruthless self-assurance of the man. But now those cold eyes were shadowed and lines of strain made the features seem almost haggard. There was a nervous tension about his whole aspect that told me he had been through a terrific grind of some sort.

"What's up?" I asked, some of his evident nervousness vaguely imparting itself to me.

"Beware of him, *sahib,*" burst forth Ali. "Have no dealings with the devil-hunted, lest the demons smell you out likewise! I say to you, *sahib*—"

"Wait!" Girtmann raised his hand; I saw that he held a peculiar-looking bundle under his other arm. He came close to me and gripped my arm with a strange passion, his eyes burning into mine. He was shaken in the clutch of some terrific excitement and I looked at him in amazement. Was this Erich Girtmann whose name was a byword for steely nerves and cynical self-control?

"You owe me your life," he was saying, speaking so hurriedly that the words tripped over each other. "I dragged you out of Lagos Bay when the sharks were ripping the shirt off of you—you've got to help me—you've got to hide me! I don't intend to lose the game after playing it this far! I'll split the proceeds with you, if you wish, but you've got to help me!"

"If you'll pull yourself together and tell me what you want," I said, "I'll be in a better position to help you. Of course, I'll do what I can for you, but you better tell me what sort of a jam you're in so I'll know how to go about it."

"Fair enough," he panted. "A drink first—gad, that heathen of yours runs like an antelope—a pretty sight we must have made galloping through the alleys—courting publicity, and that's the last thing I want—but I didn't dare let him get out of my sight or I'd have never found you—couldn't go around all over the town looking for you, not after I spied that brown-faced devil, anyhow."

I mixed him a whiskey-and-soda and offered to take his bundle while he drank, but he shook his head violently, hugging the strangely shaped packet almost fiercely. Meanwhile Ali had retired to the other side of the room in sullen silence, glaring at Girtmann in a most truculently suspicious manner.

"I thought you were dead," said I. "The rumor got about a year ago that you were killed by Bedouin bandits in the wild hill country somewhere near the Djebel Druse. Naturally, seeing you here in Djibouti was something of a surprise."

"That wasn't me the native gendarmes found stripped and mutilated," he grunted. "It was a Dutch adventurer named Stalenaus. And it wasn't Bedouins who killed him; it was Druses who thought they were getting me. The Dutchman looked quite a bit like me though, and I saw my opportunity to fade out of the picture. That night Erich Girtmann died— temporarily—and a humble Druse peddler took his place. I fooled the Druses themselves—and others!" he laughed rather wildly.

"That's why I'm in Djibouti tonight, fleeing for my life," he continued. "I'm playing a desperate game with monstrous stakes: my life against a fortune that would shame the riches of King Solomon!"

His eyes were blazing and from his wild talk I concluded that he had had a touch of the sun.

"Look here!" he cried, smiting the bundle, which gave out a metallic clink. "What do you think I have here? You'd never guess! It's wealth beyond all dreams of avarice! Gold that was taken from the mines of Ophir in the days of Solomon! Jewels that shone on the crowns of Assyria's kings! Here's riches, power, the lordship of the world!"

I stole an uneasy glance at Ali, but he merely looked back in a gloomy and pessimistic manner as if to hint that it was my own fault.

Girtmann began to undo the leather wrappings.

"I'll show you," he said hastily. "Put your boy at that outer window; I don't want anybody climbing up the wall and looking over the sill—"

The man was evidently mad, but I motioned Ali to humor him. Girtmann tore off the last wrappings and triumphantly held up to my gaze a bizarre and fantastic object. I heard Ali give a strangled cry of pure horror, but I saw nothing shocking about the object. It was an image of brass, carved in the shape of a peacock, not very large, and worked with exquisite skill; pure gold was inlaid along the wings and the tip of the spreading tail. The claws were spread as if to grip some support.

Girtmann's face was distorted with his strange gloating triumph.

"Look at it!" he exclaimed. "Glut your eyes on it! You are the first white man who has looked on it, besides myself!"

I extended a hand to examine it more closely, but Ali cried out fiercely and, leaping forward, struck my hand down.

"Because you are doomed, there is no need that you should drag my master into your own ruin," he shouted at Girtmann. "Touch it not, *sahib,* as you value your soul. It is death for a Christian or a Moslem to lay hand on that accursed thing! Allah defend us, it is Melek Taus himself this fool has stolen!"

"Melek Taus!" Recognition burst upon me and I stood aghast. "Great God, Girtmann, do you mean to tell me that this thing is the veritable brazen peacock worshipped by those unspeakable devil-worshippers, the Yezidees?"

"The same!" he was momentarily drunk with vanity and exultation. "Melek Taus, that all the Moslem world and all the Christians of the Orient fear and hate.

You've heard, then, of the Yezidees?"

"I've heard many wild tales," I answered. "Who, in the East, hasn't heard them? I've heard of that sect which worships the veritable Devil, Satan, or to give him their name, Shaitan. The legends say that seven towers link Mount Lalesh with Manchuria. These towers are the earthly abiding place of Shaitan, and gleams of light flash back and forth between them, weaving spells of evil for the sons of men. I have heard that their stronghold is in the hill-town of Sheikh-Adi, beyond Mosul, and that they worship this brazen image as the symbol of Shaitan, and to it they offer up human sacrifices in great caverns below the temple."

Girtmann nodded. "True. A few Americans, Englishmen and Frenchmen have been to Baadri and seen the castle of the Mir Beg, the Black Pope of all the Yezidees, scowling down on the village a hundred yards below. A few have even been to Sheikh-Adi and have seen the temple which is built into the solid stone of the mountainside. But what of the real temple, which lies below?"

He laughed again in savage triumph and I heard Ali call on Allah under his breath.

"My supposed murder gave the opportunity I looked for," continued Girtmann. "I had long been seeking a means to enter the secret citadel of the devil-worshippers; now that Erich Girtmann was supposedly dead, no one would be looking for him in the disguise of a Druse peddler. As a humble Druse of no rank I could more readily gain admittance into the towns of the Yezidees for the Druses are not devil-worshippers, yet neither are they Christian or Moslem, as you know.

"So I came to Baadri driving a donkey laden with European-made trinkets, and there I stayed for weeks, before venturing on to Sheikh-Adi. I acted the part of a harmless, garrulous and kindly fool. The Yezidees despised me but had no suspicions about me. Then at last I went on to Sheikh-Adi which lies only an hour's ride from Baadri. The trail winds up through wild and rocky hills and gorges, until it halts at the fantastic town that clings to the slope of Mount Lalesh the Accursed. In one of the hundreds of empty stone huts, erected for the shelter of pilgrims, I took up my abode. At first I made no attempt to even enter the outer. temple. When I finally did so, it was with a great appearance of trepidation and reverence, and to the amusement of the Yezidees I fled screaming at the sight of the great black stone serpent which stands on its tail in the inner courtyard near the doorway.

"It is said they worship this serpent, and I have seen them perform strange rites before it, but it is not the symbol of the Dark Master they adore; that is Melek Taus, the brazen peacock, into which, their legend says, Shaitan himself long ago entered. For months I abode in Sheikh-Adi. It is a strange place and a strange people. All ideas and principles which seem right and normal to us, there are reversed. Light and the lords of light are abominable to them, to whom evil and the gods of darkness are friends and masters. A Yezidee may not speak the name of Shaitan; so it is commanded in the Black Book of their creed, the scroll dictated long ago by Satan to Sheikh-Adi, founder of the cult. If you speak the name of Shaitan before a Yezidee, he is bound to kill you, or failing that, to kill himself.

"You must not wear a blue garment or ornament, since blue is a color inimicable to Shaitan. And so on, and so on. You may speak freely of Melek Taus, however, since that is the name by which Shaitan permits himself to be discussed by his worshippers. As for the Seven Towers of Evil, I cannot say, but I have seen one of them. It is a tall, slim white tower rising above the rest of the city, and when the sun strikes it, it shoots long gleams of light in all direction. But they are merely the reflection of the sun on a great golden ball on the top of the tower, though I do not doubt that the Yezidees use this by some means as a signal tower.

"Well, by carefully masking my fierce interest behind the naive curiosity of an ignorant peddler, I managed to convince myself that the temple was merely a blind—a mask to conceal the true place of worship which must lie in the subterranean corridors below. But how to reach these tunnels without being apprehended was my problem and for months I racked my mind in vain. There was always a number of priests guarding the temple and, while they did not object to my occasional awed scrutiny of the place, I dared not show that I even suspected the existence of any lower temple or shrine.

"On certain nights a great drum throbbed and thundered in the hills and the Yezidees would file through the temple doors, a silent expectant throng. Then the outer doors would be guarded until dawn by armed warriors and no sound would come from within the temple save the steady pulsing of a drum that sounded as if it was beaten far underground, and an occasional ghastly scream. On such nights the aliens of Sheikh-Adi, such as myself, were sternly ordered, on pain of frightful torture and death, to keep to their huts.

"But at last the chance came. In the spring the Yezidees have a festival in the open, which anyone can look upon. It is called the Feast of the Tower and it is grisly enough, God knows. A white bull, bedecked with flowers, is brought to the Tower of Evil and there a vein is opened in his throat and he is led around and around the Tower until he drops and dies from weakness, and the blood spurting from his throat has dyed the base of the Tower crimson all about. All the Yezidees attend this festival and this time the temple was left unguarded. I had made my plans. I had announced my intention to depart and had loaded my few belongings on my mule. My peddler's pack was on my back as I came to gape open-mouthed at the festival of the Feast. While all were intent on the gory spectacle, I slipped away to the temple. It lay unguarded.

"I hastened through the great archway into the courtyard which gave upon the temple entrance. I went down the flight of stone steps, through the gateway and into the Courtyard of the Serpent. I passed the huge stone snake which gleams black as evil and went into the enormous stone room that was the main temple. Lighted wicks, floating in oil, illuminated the place. A row of stone columns divided the huge hall into two equal parts. There was no altar, no shrine. The room was bare. One of the walls was the sheer cliff against which the temple was built and in this wall was a door. It was not locked; stairs led down to a chamber wherein was the mausoleum of Sheikh-Adi. Another door opened from this chamber. Again I went down a flight of stone steps and this time I came into an enormous natural cavern—a gigantic thing, whose vaulted roof I could barely make out in the darkness. I heard a sound as of a river flowing swiftly and went forward cautiously, feeling my way with my tiny electric torch. After walking some time in the darkness which my slender shaft of light barely pierced, I suddenly rounded a corner and came face to face—with the real temple of the Devil-worshippers.

"The cavern widened out into a perfectly colossal

cave, lighted by torches as thick as a man's thigh, flaring in niches cut into the stone, Before me a crimson and horrific altar loomed, a grisly thing of some sort of red stone, stained darkly and flanked with rows of grinning skulls laid out in curious designs. Somewhere back in the darkness of that great shadowy cavern, beyond the flickering light of the torches, a mysterious, subterranean river plunged and gurgled. Altogether it was a hideous place, and I shuddered to think what my fate would be if caught there.

"But I saw what I had come for. With its claws gripping a golden bar set into the stone of the altar stood—Melek Taus! I sprang forward and, seizing the image, wrenched it quickly from its roost—and as I did, with a grating and grinding of hinges and bolts, a section of the floor slid back behind the altar, revealing a crypt beneath! Gazing through the bars which guarded the chamber, I caught my breath. The flickering torchlight gleamed on the wealth of Araby and the Indies! My starting eyes beheld huge heaps of shimmering golden coins that must have dated back to the days of Alexander the Great; flaming gems, diamonds, rubies, emeralds, sapphires, topazes, all heaped in careless confusion—the treasure of the Yezidees!

"I dared not take time to solve the mystery of the bars. I had been in the vaults longer than I should have been already. I seized the bar from which I had torn the peacock and pulled on it; the section of the floor slid back in place. Then putting Melek Taus in my peddler's pack, I hastened back the way I had come. I was not an instant too soon. As I emerged into the upper temple, I heard a priest entering. The festival of the Feast was over.

"The priest came down the hall, but the row of

columns was between us. I slipped along in the dim gloom, keeping the columns between us, and gained the outer courtyard without being seen. But there I was accosted by a lesser priest who asked me suspiciously what I was doing loitering about the temple. He had seen me at the Feast of the Tower. I answered that I was preparing to leave Sheikh-Adi and had come to say farewell to the head priest and offer him a poor peddler's blessings for the kindness he had shown me.

"This seemed to satisfy the priest, but a bad mistake of mine aroused his suspicions. As I left the temple, to hide my nervousness—and I defy anyone to pass through such an experience and not be a little nervous!—I lit a cigarette, then thoughtlessly cast down the burning match and trod on it to extinguish it. Instantly I saw the priest's eyes narrow with sudden doubt. I cursed myself. Fire is sacred to Melek Taus and it is forbidden to spit in a flame or to tread on a flame. No Oriental would have made that mistake in Sheikh-Adi; even a Moslem would have had his wits about him and refrained from infuriating the Yezidees.

"I hastened on down the hill, and let a number of Yezidees see me untie my donkey from in front of my door, then seem to change my mind, tie him again and enter my hut. That saved my life, for I know that shortly afterward the priest came seeking me and was told I was still in my hut—was not my laden donkey tied in front of the door? So the priest waited a bit until I should come out, wishing to trap me and not alarm me by showing his suspicion, and by that time I was far away. Going into my hut I slipped out through a crevice in the rear which let into a thick clump of bushes. Wriggling through I slipped down the slope, stole a horse I found and rode like mad.

"They were not many hours behind me when I rode into Mosul; my horse dropped dead at the outskirts of the city. At Mosul I changed my disguise; I became a staid and respectable Turkish merchant. And I made a bold leap—left Mosul in the night and made straight across country for Damascus—a desperate move considering the turbulent state of the country. But thanks to my disguise I made it. But somehow my hunters got on my track and they hunted me to the very gates of Damascus—but I didn't know it then. At Damascus I changed again—back into my normal being. Erich Girtmann came to life. I believed that this move would baffle my pursuers completely. I did not then know the full extent of the Yezidee nature, the tireless, relentless hate that keeps them like blood-hounds on the trail of an enemy—God, there was a Buddhist priest who eluded them for thirty years, but in the end—

"Well, on the verge of my departure from Damascus I found that I had not fooled my enemies; by changing back into my real personality I had but betrayed to them the true identity of the man they pursued, and that must have fanned the flames of their fury for Erich Girtmann is not well loved in Syria. But I went into hiding; I have friends in Damascus. I baffled them after all. They could not find me. But a certain Damascene merchant, a friend of mine, brought me word that a Yezidee answering the description of the minor priest Yurzed had been seen lurking about the wharfs in Beirut. They expected me to hasten to the nearest western port, and since they could not find me in Damascus, they intended waiting for me. But I crossed them; I felt sure that they had all other ports guarded— Haifa, Yaffa, El Arish and Said—and I fled to

Jerusalem. There I rested a spell, until some second sense warned me that my foes were again close at hand. And I saw a Yezidee peering at me in the bazaar. That night I fled again; disguised as a Bedouin I raced southward on a racing camel.

"My enemies were hard at my heels. God—the grinding grill of that fearful hunt! I rode day and night without ceasing; once they were so near I could hear the grunting of their camels. But I eluded them, more by luck than skill, and finally came to a little village on the shore of the Red Sea. There I once more became Erich Girtmann and went as a passenger on a vile-smelling Arab dhow which cruised about the Sea on shady business.

"This morning I landed and came ashore at Djibouti. I didn't know you were here, John Mulcahy, until I saw Ali. Then while I was talking to him—God! I saw the scarred face of Yurzed among the crowded bazaar! I don't believe he saw me—my one bit of luck—but after he had passed, I was fool enough to whisper his name and nature to your idiotic Arab and the fool turned the color of ashes and started sprinting along the back alleys. I had to keep up with him, because I had to find you; but I'm betting it attracted the attention of people who will tell my enemies."

"I'll help you all I'm able," I said. "But what do you mean to do?"

"Get in hiding," he exclaimed fiercely. "Somewhere where they can't find me, not even those human bloodhounds! Then I'll enter into negotiations with them—never mind how! I have friends in the East—I have their idol—they'll pay high to get it back—and pay high they shall! The ransom of Melek Taus will be every coin, every silver ingot, every pinch of gold dust, every jewel I saw in that crypt below the altar!"

"Girtmann, you're mad!" I exclaimed sharply. "They'll never pay that sum!"

"They'll pay," his eyes burned with ferocious avarice. "This brazen thing is their god; they must get it back regardless of all cost. Oh, they'll try to kill me first, just as they've tried ever since the day I stole the idol. But I'll outwit them. I'm the shrewder and I'll prove it."

"Well," I said slowly, "to my mind it's rather a rotten thing to do, in the first place. Admitting the hideous infamy of the cult, still if you use that superstition to acquire you a fortune, you're no better than one of the members."

"I didn't ask for your opinion," he grunted. "I take what I want, and I let nothing stand in my way—cult, creed, or principle. You were always a fool, John Mulcahy, a weakling in spite of your iron body. Well, you can round out a mediocre life in poverty if you wish; not Erich Girtmann. I'm not interested in what you think of me. What I want to know is, are you going to help me out of this jam?"

"Yes, I am," I answered shortly. "After all you're a white man—at least your hide is white—and I owe you a debt. I usually pay my obligations. What do you want me to do?"

"Get me some clothes—some garments of your Arab will do," he said swiftly. "I'll disguise myself again, slip out of the hotel tonight by the servant's entrance. Send your Arab to get me a horse and have it waiting outside the city. I'll ride to that ruined fortress that lies a mile outside the city. I'll hide there."

"What!" I exclaimed. "That's madness! They'll find you and butcher you. Stay in my apartments. Here in the midst of the city, with Ali and I to keep watch, you'll have a chance."

He shook his head. "You don't know these devils. They can kill a man and never wake his bedfellow. They can strike down a man in the midst of an army. No, they'll be looking for me in the city. I'll fool them again. They'll never think of looking for me in the old fort. I'll slip out there tonight and hide. You'll have to get food out to me every now and then—but you'll have to be careful, because they'll likely be watching this hotel, in case they managed to track me here. It won't be long; the British steamer *Nagpur* is overdue. You must arrange for a passage; get it in your own name and have your things at the docks—in the last minute we'll switch and I'll slip aboard. We'll fool those devils yet! You understand you're taking a risk too—but I'll pay you well. Once I squeeze the treasure out of them, I'll see that you get a fat slice of it."

"I don't want your treasure," I answered shortly. "You couldn't hire me to do this; I'm doing it simply because you saved my life once—and I pay my debts."

He merely grunted. When I turned to tell Ali to get some of his garments, the Arab started to remonstrate, then made a gesture of true Moslem fatalism and obeyed without a word. Arrayed in flowing turboush, turban and sandals, Girtmann looked like a true Arab, an effect heightened by his hooked nose and hard black eyes. Years of travelling in the East had schooled him in his part and even Ali grunted in grudging admiration. If Girtmann had played the Druse as well as he played the Arab, no wonder he had fooled even those masters of subtlety on Mount Lalesh.

He and Ali watched closely from a small window before he glided out through the servant's entrance and vanished like a white-clad ghost in the alleys. He took with him the peacock, a supply of food and wine, and a heavy automatic pistol in a shoulder holster.

"No doubt he has gotten clean away," Ali growled to me. "The Devil watches over such rogues, even though he has stolen the Devil's demon-bird. It is you and I, *sahib*, who will be like to get our throats cut. The Yezidees will track him here, if they have not already done so. I was seen with him in the bazaar. We are doomed, *sahib!* The Devil-worshippers will come seeking him and will slay us instead. Have you not heard tales of them?"

And he regaled me with story after story, all dealing on the diabolism and atrocities of the Yezidees, some logical enough and some so extravagant of fancy that I could not control my laughter, to Ali's infinite disgust.

The next night the question arose as to food for Girtmann and Ali and I argued over who should take it to him.

"You were seen with him," said I. "The natural thing for the Yezidees to do would be to follow you. On the other hand I have not been seen in connection with him and I had better take the food to him."

"Rest assured those devils have connected us both with him," answered Ali pessimistically. "You are subtle as a bull elephant and stealthy as an army. I will hide my face and slip out the servant's door as did he."

So he did and returned with the word that Girtmann was safely ensconced in the old crumbling fortress, "among the rats and lizards," and believed he had finally given his implacable enemies the slip. As for me, I was beginning to believe most of his terror emanated from his own guilty conscience. I had not seen a Yezidee, nor any sign of one. Doubtless Girtmann only thought he recognized a priest of that fearsome cult in the bazaar.

But Ali shook his head gloomily. "They watch us," he answered. "Thrice have I seen a shadow flitting among the alleys outside this hotel; they will not show themselves till they are ready to strike—and then they will strike silently. I evaded them; I think they believe Girtmann to be still in your apartments, but in their own good time they will cut our throats. And they will hunt down Girtmann and slay him, too."

That steamer continued to be overdue. Again Ali stole forth to carry food and wine to Girtmann. He slipped out just after dusk, and close upon midnight I heard a stealthy, sandalled step in the corridor. A key turned in the lock and a figure entered; I recognized the flowing turboush and the turban end which concealed all the face except the blazing eyes. Those eyes—something unfamiliar about them struck me— and that figure—Ali was not that tall! And then stark unreasoning terror gripped me as the man flung aside the turban end and laughed, hideously and soundlessly, in my face. It was not so much physical terror of the lean vulture-like stranger who stood before me in Ali's garments, but the whole thing seemed so unreal it smacked of sorcery.

Still laughing in frightful, silent mockery and triumph, the Yezidee drew from beneath his robes a heavy pistol which he levelled at my heart. His left hand groped among his garments. And I awoke from the trance of horror which gripped me and hurled myself on him, staking all on the desperate chance that he would not dare fire lest the shot arouse the people of the hotel. I was right. Instead of pulling the trigger, he lifted the weapon and struck at me savagely with the barrel. A stunning blow had it landed solidly; as it was it staggered me and filled my vision with points of flying light.

But the next instant I had gripped him like a grizzly and he could not break my hold. It was a knife he gripped in his left hand and he dropped the pistol and devoted all his attention to driving the long cruel blade into my heart. We tumbled about on the floor, fighting silently except for our labored breathing. He was lean and hard as a wolf, as tall as I though not so heavy, and possessed of steel spring thews. Once he almost got a gouging thumb in my eye and again he sank his fang-like teeth into my arm so the blood started.

We reeled upright, somehow, still close-clinched, and he drove his knee to my groin. Maddened by the pain I wrenched savagely at his wrist and felt the bone snap between my fingers. He groaned and momentarily relaxed and in that instant I tore loose and crashed my right fist to his jaw with every ounce of my beef behind it. He dropped like a log and lay without twitching.

Without another glance at him, but gasping for breath, I caught up my helmet, buckled on a heavy pistol and took up a double-barrelled ten-bore shotgun. I was in the game, up to the hilt, and I was resolved to play it out, whatever hand Fate dealt me. As I went out the door I glanced at the Yezidee and saw that he was regaining consciousness.

Down in the compound I awoke an amazed and volubly resentful servant who sleepily brought out and saddled my horse. In a few minutes more I was riding recklessly through the narrow winding streets. Djibouti lay silent beneath the stars; my steed's drumming hoofs waked eerie echoes. Of plans I had but one: to ride as swiftly as I could to the deserted fortress. That both Girtmann and Ali were dead, I felt certain, and a slow relentless wrath burned in me. I owed a debt to Girtmann; a greater debt to Ali. If Girtmann had saved my life once, Ali had saved me half a dozen times from Bedouin bullets, Taureg scimitars, Matabele spears—

he was more than a servant; he was a tried and trusty friend. And now he had fallen victim to a foul brood of demon-worshippers, aiding a man whom he hated, but aided because the man claimed friendship to me. I cursed as I rode and the veins throbbed in my temples. If I could not rescue, I could revenge, by Satan!

The silent town fell away behind me and now across the scrub-strewn waste I saw loom the dark and mysterious pile of stone that was the ruined fortress. A relic of Arab rule it was, and once commanded the city of Djibouti with its frowning cannon whose flaring muzzles were piously inscribed with Koranic verses.

A few hundred yards from the ruin I dismounted and tied my horse in a dense thicket, stealing forward on foot. Dense clouds masked the moon and it was very dark. I groped forward and finally came into the ancient courtyard, or compound, feeling under my feet the cracked slabs through which dense weeds and vines pushed up. All was silent. The moon showed a hint of breaking through and I hastened into the shadow of a moldering wall. A crumbling stairway showed near at hand and up it I went, hugging the shadows. The moon came out clear now and flung the black shadows into bold relief. I came into a corridor, dusty and bat-haunted, eerily lighted by the moonbeams which flowed through the long fallen roof. I stole along it, feeling uncomfortably as if I were stalking blindly into a trap, when ahead of me I saw a tiny gleam of light. I remembered Ali saying that there were chambers in the old fortress almost intact in spite of the ravages of time. I stole forward. The light emanated from a small crevice in the wall. Cautiously I placed my eye thereto.

I was looking into one of the more intact chambers. It was dusty and ancient and showed signs that owls had nested, and jackals laired, there, but the walls were solid and the roof not altogether fallen down. It was lighted by a candle stuck on the wall and ten men were in the room. I saw Girtmann first; he was bound hand and foot, a rope about his body holding him upright to a ring set in the wall. He was apparently unharmed, but his eyes blazed in the candlelight with fear, rage and hate; he was like a trapped wolf. Flung carelessly on the floor, likewise bound and naked save for his loin-cloth, was Ali; blood was dried on a wound in his scalp, but he was conscious. The other eight were Yezidees. No doubt about that. They were tall, lean and rangy with evil, vulture-like faces.

One, a scarred-faced devil I knew must be Yurzed, was speaking in Kurdish. "You are doomed, man; you have laid the hands of sacrilege on Melek Taus and not all the hosts of God could save you. But you will save yourself much torture if you will tell us where you have hidden Melek Taus."

"You dare not kill me," snarled Girtmann, "for then you would lose your idol forever. Only I know where it is hidden."

I had no time to waste listening to the conversation. I saw the chamber had two doors and a window; the doors were in the end walls, and the window in the wall opposite the crevice through which I gazed. I believed that the door to the left opened upon a landing and a stair, and perhaps the door to the right did also. At any rate, I stole quickly down the corridor seeking a door or chamber that could let me into the other chamber.

I gained a courtyard again, an inner courtyard, dark as a well. Above I saw a faint gleam of light that marked the chamber I wished to reach, shining through the silks that had been hung across the broken window. I stole past the crumbling stairway without attempting to mount it. I felt that it was well guarded. I

would enter the building on the opposite side of the
court and was sure I would find a stair that would let
me into the upper corridors. I wanted to come upon the
Yezidees from the unguarded door.

As I stole past the stairs I glanced up and halted
short, tensed, thinking to have glimpsed a sudden
sinister movement in the shadows halfway up the
broken stairs. I strained my eyes, but the stairway,
hanging to the overhanging walls, was a well of
darkness. I passed on swiftly. And now I was halfway
across the courtyard, and a sudden stealthy sound
made me whirl, electrified.

The moon was out and in its light I saw a horrific
shape, apparently poised in midair; in full mid-leap I
saw him, the lean figure, the loose garments spread like
the wings of a gigantic bat, the hideous face contorted
with passion and bloodlust, the gleaming knife held
high in a dusky hand—all this I caught in one flashing,
horrified glimpse, even as I acted instinctively. There
was no time for conscious thought; even as I whirled I
fired from the hip and the blast caught and crumpled
the leaping Yezidee in midair, literally blowing him
from the very muzzle.

The crash of the heavy shotgun reverberated
through the ruined fortress terrifically, waking
cataclysmic echoes, and a fierce shout sounded from
above. Light streamed suddenly from the window as
the silks were thrust aside and I could visualize savage
eyes peering out and down. But even while the echoes
of my shot were thundering through the ruins, I had
leaped into the shadows of the wall and crouched there,
unseen by the watchers from above. The moon was
hidden again and I doubted if even the keen eyes of the
devil-worshippers could recognize the shattered shape

which lay, like a bundle of tattered clothes, at the foot of the wall.

The silks fell back in place and, straining my ears, I heard the unmistakable sound of men moving above. And I took a desperate chance. It was evident that the Yezidees were stealing down to investigate the shot. Those remaining in the torture chamber would be triply on guard, doubtless watching both doors. I laid down my shotgun and began climbing the wall. It would have been an impossible feat except for the fact that the crumbling of the wall had left deep crevices in it and jutting stones. As I mounted I twisted my head about to see shadowy figures glide from the well of the stairway. My flesh crawled and my hair bristled to think how helpless I would be, clinging like a spider on the wall, if they spied me. But they had sighted the shot-riddled body of the man I had killed and they clustered about him, as I could see dimly. Then I reached the window and drew myself up to the ledge.

Most of the bars had long fallen out; I looked through the silks and my heart leaped. Only one Yezidee remained guarding the room, a big, sombre devil with a pistol in one hand and a scimitar in the other. He was paying no attention to the window—in fact he had his back to it. His gaze flickered from one door to the other. Holding my breath I drew myself over the sill—and as I was half over, he whirled and his eyes blazed.

Our shots crashed at the same instant and it was pure luck that saved me, because there was no time to aim. His bullet cut a lock of hair from my head and, through the smoke of our fire, I saw him sway and crumple limply. The next instant I was in the chamber and bending over Ali.

"Sahib!" he stammered wildly. *"Allaho akbar!* I knew—I knew you would come—"

Working frenziedly with one eye on the doors, I freed him and he sprang up and caught up the scimitar of the fallen Yezidee. That he was weak and stiff from his bonds and from loss of blood was evident, but his eyes flashed with murderous anger. I freed Girtmann and gave him the pistol the Yezidee had used. He spoke no word of thanks, but he grinned fiercely and without mirth: "They'll never get the peacock, the filthy dogs!"

Outside the silence was sinister, breathless.

"What happened, Ali?" I asked swiftly.

"I walked into a trap," he answered. "I saw naught, heard naught, but as I entered the shadows of the fortress, a shadow rose from the darkness and struck me senseless. When I came to my senses I was bound and stripped, and lay on the chamber floor—"

"They'd got me, too," growled Girtmann. "Caught me with a trick as old in the East as Egypt: I heard a racket in the courtyard and was fool enough to look out the window. One of them was on the roof and he threw a noose over my head and choked me unconscious. How did you get here? They dressed one of their murderers in Ali's clothes and sent him to get you."

"Never mind," I answered, "we've got to get out of here. They're planning some deviltry and this room isn't one we can defend against a rush. We've got to take a chance of slipping out. Out in the open, away from these ruins, we've a fighting chance. Here we're caught like rats in a trap."

"Wait!" Girtmann sprang to the ring in the wall and twisted it powerfully; with a creak of rusty bolts a portion of the wall slid away, disclosing a dull glint of

brass. Girtmann took from the secret niche the brazen
peacock.

"The fools," he grunted, "had me tied to the very key
of the puzzle and didn't know it. I discovered that niche
the first night I was hiding here. All right, let's go."

"Wait," I cautioned him. "If we try to go down those
stairs, they'll pick us off in the dark. I'll scout a bit
through this other door; I don't believe they can reach
us from the courtyard by that direction. Girtmann, you
watch the stair and Ali, keep your attention on that
window."

I went through the door, coming into a wide, dusty
chamber; through this I went and into a corridor. I
groped my way along in the dark, cocked revolver held
in front of me, and my skin crawling in anticipation of
a sudden and silent knife-thrust. Then I came into the
moonlight and swore. I had come to the end of the
corridor. Through the fallen roof and shattered walls
the vagrant moon, now clear, shone brightly. And no
stair led down.

Somewhere back along the corridor I knew there
must be a door or chamber letting into the parallel
corridor into which I had first come. There were two
choices: either make our way into that other corridor
and down the crumbling stair I had first ascended; or
essay to climb down the wall at the end of this corridor,
a task I could see at a glance would be much more
difficult than climbing the courtyard wall. I froze
suddenly as a hideous scream split the silence, and hard
on its fearsome echoes came the clash of steel and the
fierce yells of fighting men.

I whirled and raced recklessly back the way I had
come, leaping into the chamber. A bloodcurdling sight
met my eyes. Girtmann lay sprawled in a pool of blood
on the floor and but a glance was needed to tell that he

was dead; from his throat protruded the ivory hilt of a thin, wicked dagger. And backed against the wall was Ali, fighting in wild beast desperation for his life against a group of lean, snarling devils led by a tall, scarred swordsman—Yurzed. Ali's scimitar leaped and flickered like a living thing, but it was evident that only a matter of seconds lay between him and extinction; he could not long keep at bay those licking, dancing blades. Fools that we were, we had forgotten the broken roof; through it the Yezidees had come.

I threw up my revolver to fire, then sudden inspiration struck me. On the floor, at the very edge of the grisly pool whose slowly widening tide dabbled its wings in crimson, lay the brazen peacock. With a swift stride I reached it and placed the revolver's muzzle within a few inches of it. If I pulled the trigger, the bullet would shatter the frail image at that range. The Yezidees whirled and stood frozen, while Ali fell back against the window sill, panting and gasping.

"One move and I blast your god into bits of metal," I said grimly. "I will bargain for our lives—our lives against Melek Taus."

"You cannot live," said Yurzed. "You have committed the sacrilege unspeakable."

"The *sahib* has not touched your accursed idol," said Ali. "Nor have I; only he—" pointing at the corpse on the floor. "And he has paid the penalty."

"Then give us Melek Taus and we will go in peace," said Yurzed.

"I'd prefer to see you hanged for murder," I growled. "How can I trust you?"

"I swear not to harm either of you, now or later," said the priest, raising his hand with a certain impressiveness. "I swear by the wings of Melek Taus, by the Seven Towers of Evil, by the beard of Sheikh-

Adi, by the sceptre of the Mir Beg, by the Serpent of Wisdom, by the Nameless Name of all Names."

Ali flung down his scimitar. "Be at ease, *sahib,*" he said. "No spawn of Hell dare break that oath. Take up your demon-bird, dogs, and begone."

And Yurzed, sheathing his scimitar, reverentially took up the brazen thing and wrapped it in his long cloak. Then, salaaming to us, the Devil-worshippers went noiselessly into the night. No sound came back to mark their going; it was as if they had come from night and nowhere like a band of specters. And like phantoms they vanished.

The Black Bear
Bites

Night hung over the river like a sullen threat, pregnant with doom. I crouched in the straggling bushes and shivered in the dampness. Somewhere in the great dark house in front of me, a gong sounded faintly—once. Eight times that gong had sounded since I had hidden there. I had counted the notes mechanically. I watched the shadowed bulk of the house grimly. House of mystery it was—the house of the mysterious Yotai Yun, the Chinese merchant prince—and what unsavory business went on within its brooding walls no white man knew. Bill Lannon had wondered—ex-secret service man of the British Empire, and swift to revert to old ways. He had made secret investigations of his known—had spoken to me vaguely of grim things hidden behind the walls of Yotai Yun's house—had hinted to me and to Eric Brand of mysterious gatherings, deep plots and a terrible Hooded Monk of some dark cult who promised a yellow empire.

Eric Brand, lean, reckless-eyed adventurer, had laughed at Lannon, but I had not. I knew the lad was

149

like a hunting hound on the trail of something sinister and mysterious. He had told us one night—the three of us sitting in the European Club and sipping our whiskey-and-sodas, that he meant to slip into Yotai Yun's house that night to learn what was going on there. They found his body next morning, rolling limply in the wash of the Yangtze's filthy yellow tide, with a thin dagger hilt-deep between his shoulders.

Bill Lannon was my friend. That was why I was crouching in the thin bushes in the hours past midnight, watching the house of Yotai Yun, where it loomed just beyond the ragged outskirts of Hankow. And I wondered what Bill Lannon had found before they butchered him and flung him to the fishes; was it piracy, smuggling, or sedition on a huge scale that was being plotted in that dark house? That Yotai Yun dealt in shady commerce and crooked river business, all knew; but none had ever been able to pin anything on him.

Through the mist loomed suddenly a tall, shuffling figure—a native, wrapped in shapeless garments. He made his way toward a squalid, deserted looking fishing hut that perched on the bank of the river, perhaps fifty yards from the wall that surrounded the great house. I stiffened suddenly. Eight men had gone into that hut while I lay watching; none had come out. Once or twice I had thought to see a glimmer of light within the hut, but to all outward appearances it was absolutely vacant. And each time, soon after the native had disappeared into the hut, the gong had sounded from somewhere within the Dragon House. Eight men had gone into the hut; eight times the gong had sounded in the house. What was the connection between that sordid, ruined fisher's hut and the palace-like dwelling of Yotai Yun?

The native approached the ruined door and I rose from my covert and followed him swiftly and recklessly. Had he turned he could not have failed to have seen me. But he went in without a backward look, pulling the sagging door to behind him. I stole to the wall and peered through a crack. All was utter darkness within the hut, but presently a match was struck and I saw the native crouching in the middle of the floor. I looked for the eight men who had preceded him; the hut was empty but for that one native! He moved some rags aside on the floor and struck on the floor with his knuckles—three times—then paused—struck thrice more—paused—then struck three more times.

The match had gone out, but a sudden thin square of light formed in the hut floor; it widened as a trapdoor was thrust up and a villainous yellow face was framed in the aperture. No words were exchanged; the doorkeeper merely nodded and withdrew and the newcomer clambered down into the trap. As he did his features were clearly limned and I recognized him—a well known river-pirate, long wanted by the authorities for robbery and murder. He vanished and the trapdoor slipped back in place again. Now I began to sense the connection. Evidently that secret door let into a tunnel which connected the hut with the Dragon House. The gong was used to announce the coming of the men who used that mode of entry. Why, I was determined to learn.

I entered the hut swiftly and stealthily and, feeling with my hands in the darkness, located the contour of the trapdoor, and knocked as the Chinaman had done. Almost instantly the trapdoor began to rise and I crouched quickly behind it. Again the wicked yellow face appeared, and beady eyes darted about as the owner failed to discover me where I crouched behind his head. He half emerged from the trap—and before he could turn and locate me, I caught his throat in a grip that strangled the yell in his gullet, and crashed my right fist behind his ear. He sagged in my grasp, out cold.

I dragged him out of the aperture, and bound and gagged him with strips torn from his garments. Then I laid him in a dingy corner of the hut and hid him under some dirty rags that I found on the floor. Then I drew my pistol, a .45 automatic, and cautiously descended the trap, closing the secret door behind me. Where I was going, what I was to do, I had no idea; but I knew that the trail of vengeance led somehow straight to Yotai Yun, and that was the trail I had sworn to follow to the bitter end.

Stone steps led down into a narrow, stone-walled tunnel that ran straight, as near as I could tell, for the Dragon House. It was fairly well lighted with lanterns hung at regular intervals, and I went along it swiftly but warily, gun ready. But I saw no one and after a time I believed I was directly under the great house; and then the tunnel ended in a stout wooden door. I tried it cautiously, my nerves on edge, not knowing what might lie on the other side. It gave under my fingers and swung inward, disclosing a wide chamber, with floor, walls and ceiling of stone. A rough table and some chairs, suggestive of European manners, adorned the otherwise bare chamber, but it was empty of humans.

I entered, closing the door behind me. Across the room in front of me I saw a stone stairway leading up, and beside the foot of the stair, a small door. I had started up the stair when I heard a sudden murmur of voices above me and the trapdoor at the top of the stairs began to open. I hastily sprang from the stairs and jerked at the small door. It opened and I slipped in, not a second too soon. Someone was descending the stair and I heard the staccato babble of Oriental conversation.

I had no idea what sort of a place I had gotten into. It was as dark as the inside of a cat. As I groped about, expecting to fall into a pit or get a sudden knife in the back, I found myself wondering what Eric Brand would say if my body was found floating in the Yangtze the next day. He had predicted that end for Bill Lannon, warning him, in his cynical way, to avoid meddling in Oriental affairs. I never liked Brand as Lannon had liked him, and had never made a confidant of him; that supercilious, sophisticated clubman was too listless in his attitude toward life, for me. His attitude toward human values differed from mine; he affected to despise all human effort and ambitions and emotions. Well, I'm but a rough sailorman, uncultured and untaught in sophist ways, and my cult is an eye for an eye, a tooth for a tooth. And that's why I was stalking Yotai Yun that night in the silence and the mist.

By feeling along I found I was in a very narrow corridor and soon I felt what was evidently a narrow stone stair, leading up. So up I groped in the utter darkness and presently came into what I felt was another chamber, though I could see nothing and dared not strike a match. I barked my shin on a case of some sort and stumbled onto a stack of objects that brought my heart into my mouth by their sudden rattle. But nothing happened and I began to feel about. Gad, the place was a regular armory! My fingers made out stacks of rifles, cases of holstered pistols, dismantled machineguns, and cases that I knew were filled with ammunition. Revolution and uprising it could mean, no less, and I sweated in the dark as I thought of the innocent Europeans, Americans and peaceful Chinese who slept in Hankow ignorant of the peril looming over them.

I groped until I found a door about opposite, I judged, from the place I entered. There was a catch on it, but it was on the inside and I manipulated it with ease, stepping through the door into a sort of narrow corridor. A dim sort of light filtered in from somewhere and I knew what kind of a place it was— one of those secret corridors running through a wall. China's honeycombed with such, as is all the Orient, where masters spy continually on their servants and their household. I stole along until a mutter of conversation reached me from outside the corridor and I halted and began to hunt for the peephole I knew should be there. I found it quickly enough and peered through it.

I was looking into a large and ornately furnished chamber, whose walls were hung with velvet tapestries worked with dragons, gods and demons, and which was lighted by candles which shed a weird golden glow over all. On silken cushions and divans sat a strange and motley crew—respectable merchants and minor government officials jowl-and-jowl with wild, evil-visaged raggamuffins who had all the earmarks of cutthroats. I recognized the river-pirate who had preceded me into the tunnel and realized the reason for the secret entrance. Through that tunnel came outlaws and criminals who might cast suspicion on the Dragon House if they came in openly. Evidently the others, the officials and the traders, had come in openly. Altogether there were about forty of them, all Orientals—Chinese, mainly, but I saw a few Eurasians and Malays.

All were seated, watching a dais at the other end of the room. On that dais sat Yotai Yun, lean, sardonic, hawk-like, and beside him sat a tall, black-robed figure whose features were hidden in a black mask—the Hooded Lama! He was no myth then, but a savage reality. I looked at him closely; from his hood glimmered two piercing, magnetic eyes. Evil exuded from him like an aura. I shuddered involuntarily. Then he rose to his full gaunt height and began to speak, and his audience hung breathlessly on his words. His resonant voice filled the room, his gestures were imposing, commanding. Shudders of abhorrence shook me as I listened to the blasphemous utterances that poured, in stately Chinese, from his hidden lips. It was revolution he was preaching, rapine and red war! Death to all foreign devils and to all Orientals who stood in their way!

Prophet of an old and evil religion he was, of a devil-worshipping cult, the very existence of which is not dreamed of by most white men. Old, evilly old, it was, and long had it lurked in the brooding black mountains of the East. Genghis Khan had bowed before its priests, and Tamerlane, and centuries before them, Attila. Now that terrible cult, which had slumbered for so many thousands of years in the wastes of Mongolia, was rousing from its slumber, was shaking its foul mane and gazing about for victims—was stretching forth tentacles to grasp the heart of China.

And it was the part of its followers to pave the way for the new empire, said the Hooded Lama. Let them forget the false teachings of Confucius and Buddha, and the gods of Tibet, who had allowed their people to come under the yoke of the white-skinned devils. Let them rise under the leadership of the prophet the Old Ones had sent them and the great Cthulhu would sweep them all to victory. Just as Genghis Khan had trampled the world beneath his horse-hoofs, so would they trample the white devils and found a new, yellow empire that should outlast a million years.

His voice rose to a blood-frenzied scream—murder, rapine, death, hate, plunder, bloodshed! He caught up his listeners in the torrent of his own madness and they leaped and howled like mad dogs. Then he changed his mood swiftly and became cunning, crafty. The time was not yet, he said; much remained to be done. More converts were to be gained, more sedition was to be planted, more secret work to be done. The red madness faded from the eyes of his listeners to be replaced by the thoughts he had implanted in their minds—craft, patience like that of a hunting wolf, ferocious guile.

I listened in horror, realizing the extent to which this insanity might reach. China is always a powder keg, ready for a match. This unknown priest had power, persuasion, personality. Many an Oriental empire has been founded on less. I felt weak as I visualized the red events attendant on a sudden, determined uprising— all China relaxed, unsuspecting, peaceful. Blood would run in the streets; a sudden unexpected attack in force would wipe out the government troops. Hordes of malcontents and bandits would join the revolutionaries. Foreigners would be slaughtered wholesale.

The rebellion would fail, of course. The nations of the world would send their armies to protect their citizens and their interests. The revolt would be crushed in blood and slaughter, and Yotai Yun and the Black Lama would leave their heads on Peking Tower. But before that many would die, Chinese and white people. The thought of the damage to lives and property turned me sick.

Now suddenly a native rushed in, eyes blazing—

evidently the man I had heard descend into the tunnel from the house. Behind him, face contorted in rage and fear, came the man who had guarded the trapdoor in the hut. They spoke rapidly to Yotai Yun and his eyes glinted in a way that made the doorkeeper blanch. But the merchant-prince showed no perturbation. He spoke quickly to the Lama who nodded and sat down, and Yotai Yun rose and said tranquilly:

"Lords and honorable friends, there is a spy in the house; these unworthy ones have just reported. Who it is, we cannot say, but his shift will be short. Go now, without haste but without delay, each the same way he came. Later you shall be sent for again."

I turned cold all over for I knew who the spy was! The Orientals rose hurriedly and went with no more ado. In a remarkably short time the room was vacant except for Yotai Yun, the Lama who stood like a black image, and the servants who quaked before them. To them Yotai Yun spoke: "You—" to the first one, "gather the servants and search the house; find this spy as you value your life!" The servant bowed low and left the room and Yotai Yun turned to the trapdoor keeper.

"You," he said with concentrated venom, "have failed me. You whom I selected for that difficult task because of your former courage and sagacity. Bah!"

The wretched servant was shaking like a leaf.

"But Master, I have never failed before—"

"One failure is too many, dog," said Yotai Yun in a toneless voice. "I discharge you from my service!"

And whipping a small revolver from his robes, he fired point-blank. The servant fell without a groan, blood trickling from his temple. Yotai Yun clapped his hands and two big coolies entered. At a gesture from their master, they lifted the body and carried it stolidly from the room.

The Lama, who had stood motionless throughout, evincing no interest whatever, spoke to Yotai Yun and they went through a curtain-hung doorway and vanished. Believing them to have gone into an adjoining chamber, I went swiftly along the corridor until I came to the next peephole. I peered through into the room. Sure enough, there sat Yotai Yun and the Black Lama, white man fashion, at a lacquered table, drinking rice wine from amber cups thin as eggshells. I could tell nothing of the Lama's face; he raised his mask only just enough to bring the cup to his lips. They were speaking in low tones and I pressed close to the wall straining my ears. That Yotai Yun's slipper-footed servants were gliding through rooms and corridors, knives in their hands and murder in their hearts, I knew, but one part of the house seemed as safe as another, and I lingered, eavesdropping.

"You have wrought well, my friend," Yotai Yun was saying. "Your tongue makes men drunk and maddens them. You almost convince me that your mad scheme will succeed."

"That it will succeed I know," answered the Lama, and I thrilled with a sudden sense of vague familiarity—I had heard that voice somewhere—but where?

"We will succeed," continued the Masked Monk, "because the people are fat and restless—ripe for revolt. But we must work cautiously. Time—it will take time. The men who came here tonight represent the horde which waits in semi-ignorance and expectancy. Each of those men is a sedition spreader—a talker of revolt. We must be wary. Let anything happen unexpectedly, let the leaders lose faith in us, or let even one of us lose his life, and the revolt dies before it is fully born."

"We must not take too long," grunted Yotai Yun. "The coils of the government are closing about me; I feel them, though I cannot see them. The authorities have too many spies, my businesses have grown too big to keep hidden altogether. If I dared I would make a break, as the Yankees say—but I could not leave Hankow without being seized, arrested and held on suspicion. They already suspect much of my smuggling and gun-running; an attempt at flight would crystallize their suspicions. Otherwise you had not persuaded me so easily to join you."

"Safety for you and wealth for us both," said the Black Lama, filling his goblet. "When the revolt breaks the government will have its hands too full to bother about smuggling—and we will have the whole screeching horde of cutthroats behind us. Easy to watch which way the feather falls; if the revolt becomes popular with the masses and spreads all over China— well, that yellow empire I have been ranting about may prove to be no pipe dream. If not, if we see that the revolt is about to be crushed, it will be an easy matter to loot Hankow in the midst of the fighting and slip away downriver, or across country."

"I wonder at your daring and ruthlessness, Masked One," said Yotai Yun slowly. "You play a dangerous game. Did your dupes know, for instance, that you are not even a Mongolian, they would tear you to pieces. And the real priests of Yog-Sothoth; do you not fear their vengeance when they learn—as they eventually must—that you have been posing as one of their infernal cult?"

"Danger is the breath of life to me," answered the imposter with a wild laugh. "I have lost all my illusions; without the breathtaking touch-and-go of risk and adventure, I should perish of boredom. No, I do not fear the Mongolian devil-worshippers. Only one man is likely to hinder us; one man that we must put out of the way—Black John O'Donnell."

Yotai Yun nodded. "A great black bear of a man, fierce and unforgiving. But he has no craft. Why fear him?"

"I don't fear him. But he has the craft of the bear you name him, and the ferocious patience of the brute. He does not forget and his is a one-track mind that, having once taken up a trail, follows it to the bitter end, through hell and high water. That fool Lannon was his friend; and Lannon told him enough to make him suspect that you, at least, had a hand in his friend's murder. I tell you, we must kill Black John or he will find a way to kill both of us. In fact, I would not be at all surprised if he were not the 'spy' who has found entrance into the Dragon House tonight."

Yotai Yun gave a startled exclamation and half rose, drawing his pistol. The Lama laughed sardonically. "Don't be afraid. Have you no confidence in your servants? They will rout him out, wherever he's hiding; you said yourself that he has no subtlety. The secrets of this house are not known to him—"

I was pressing close to the peephole, shaken with red rage, but even in my anger, I was alert enough to hear a sudden stealthy sound behind me. It was just enough to save my life. I wheeled suddenly, in time to see, in the dim light, a glittering blade lifted above me, clenched in a yellow hand, and below that hand a face contorted into a devil's mask.

As I turned the dagger hissed toward my heart, but by blind chance I caught his wrist in my left hand, and with my clenched right I smashed him hard under the heart. He gasped and staggered, then hurled himself bodily upon me. He was a big man, big as I, and strong

as a bull—an ex-wrestler, I think. We clenched and
tore on hard-braced feet; he could not break the grip I
had on his knife-hand, and I could not free my right fist
so as to crash home a knockout blow. Sweat stood out
on his forehead and his breath hissed between his
parted lips. I was gasping myself from the struggle, but
I felt him weakening. I put forward all my effort in a
sudden explosive wrench and heave—his weakening
legs gave way suddenly and we crashed together into
the thin partition—crashed clear through it in a cloud
of plaster and a splintering of light wood, and landed
on the floor outside with a terrific impact. The
Chinaman was on the bottom and his head had gotten
twisted down somehow—I heard his neck snap like a
rotten branch as we crashed to the floor.

I looked up into the muzzles of two pistols. Raising
my hands slowly above my head I rose sullenly and
stood, with my feet wide-braced, my head sunk on my
breast, glaring at my captors from beneath my heavy
brows. My terrible hate beat through my soul in deep
red surges as I looked on the men who murdered Bill
Lannon, and only the thought of the pistol under my
left arm kept me from leaping upon them, guns and all,
with my bare hands.

"By Buddha," murmured Yotai Yun, his slant eyes
widened, "it is the black bear, after all! Lord Lama, you
were right."

The Lama laughed sardonically. "Black John
O'Donnell it is, right enough! He was not slow in taking
the trail. I think he has killed your servant, who was
fool enough to come to grips with the bear! But
summon your men and we'll soon have this obstacle
out of our way."

"You damned swine," I growled. "You killed Bill
Lannon—and you hold the upper hand at the moment;

but the game's not played out yet, by thunder!"

"Not quite, but almost," answered the Lama, as Yotai Yun clapped his hands. "It but remains a quick dagger thrust and the splash of a corpse in the river— and the big black bear will bite no more!"

Seven or eight big Chinese entered—hard-faced, wicked-eyed men, with daggers and bludgeons in their hands. Yotai Yun nodded toward me.

"Dispose of him," he said, as if he were speaking of a hog or a beef.

They approached me and I backed slowly away, hands still high. Yotai Yun and the Lama still had their guns trained on me, and the servants were closing in in a sort of half circle, herding me toward an outer door. I gathered that they intended butchering me in some other part of the house. I backed slowly toward the door; a sidelong glance showed that it was open. The Lama and Yotai Yun stood side by side, and Yotai Yun was laughing at me. A big Chinese caught me roughly by the shirt-front with one hand, pricking me with a knife he held in the other. And like a flash I moved.

I've taken many a man by surprise; no one expects me to be half as quick as I am, because of my bulk. I swept the Chinaman off his feet and, with the same motion, hurled him bodily against Yotai Yun and the Lama. The three went down in a heap, Yotai Yun firing as he fell. The bullet snapped past my ear, but I was already leaping for the door. The whole pack was howling and hacking at my heels, but I was through the door by a flashing fraction of a second the quicker, and I slammed it in their faces, bracing myself to hold it against their frenzied efforts until I could slam in place the bolt I found on the other side.

Then I turned quickly. The door was splintering swiftly under the assault of my pursuers and I knew it would stand only for a moment or so. I heard the furious voices of Yotai Yun and the Lama urging their minions on. I was standing in a wide chamber, much like that I had just left, and on the opposite side there was a closed door. The walls were hung with heavy tapestries, as in the other rooms. I crossed the room swiftly and hurled the door open. Into what sort of chamber or corridor it let, I did not stop to see. I was not seeking escape, but vengeance. Drawing my pistol I concealed myself behind the hangings on the wall, just as the door crashed inward. The horde flooded through howling like mad dogs and brandishing their blades. Seeing the other door open, they leaped to the natural conclusion that I had escaped by that route and, rushing across the room, crowded through the doorway. I heard the sound of their flying feet dwindle away down some corridor. Behind them came Yotai Yun and the Lama, half running, but left behind by their followers' mad dash. I grinned wolfishly; all was coming about as I had hoped.

The two had reached the outer door when I leaped from the hangings and growled: "Turn, you swine, and take it from the front!"

Taken by sudden surprise though they were, they whirled firing. I heard the spat of their bullets and I felt their impact, but my gun, too, was blazing and the Black Lama dropped like an empty sack and lay still. Yotai Yun reeled back as though struck by an invisible hammer, clutched at the hangings with a bloody hand, fired his last shot point-blank and, as my third bullet tore through his body, slumped to the floor and lay twitching.

I knew I had plenty of lead in me; at that range there could be little missing. My left leg felt numb from the thigh down, my left arm and shoulder were rapidly growing stiff, and blood was trickling down my breast. And I could hear the Chinese coming back along the corridor, shouting and clashing their weapons. They had heard the shots and turned back. And I had to meet them, crippled and with a half-empty gun. But I grinned with savage mirth. I had accomplished my design; my foes lay stark before my feet and Bill Lannon was avenged. I'd paid that debt and had no regrets. Sooner or later, a man must die anyway.

The yellow pack came howling through the door and *I gripped the tapestries to steady myself and emptied my gun into the thick of them.* The foremost went down in a windrow and the rest drew back, aghast. I could hear them whispering and jabbering outside the chamber; I could hear the slap-pad of slippered feet and the rattle of blades. Weakness began to steal over me and my left arm felt dead. I shook my head to clear it and the red drops spattered.

"Come in and have it over, you yellow devils!" I roared, fearing that if they did not rush me quickly, my weakness would bowl me over and I would be butchered like a sheep without a chance to strike a blow.

Then suddenly the room was flooded with men from the other door. One of them approached me and I struck at him viciously with my empty gun before I saw he wore the uniform of the Chinese constabulary.

"Easy, my friend," he said soothingly. "We are friends—do you not know me?"

"Oh, it's you, Kang Yao," I said dizzily. "Sorry—blood in my eyes; let me sit down."

He guided my blundering steps to a divan. Looking about I saw the room was full of native police and soldiers. They had herded up Yotai Yun's servants, who stood about, manacled and with sullen resignation. Kang Yao bent over the two plotters. The Black Lama had been hit only once, but he was stone dead. Yotai Yun had three bullets through him, but he was still conscious.

His eyes roved to the still form of his partner in crime and a sardonic smile twisted his pallid lips.

"One man can overthrow an unborn empire," he whispered. "We laughed at the black bear—but the black bear has bitten us both—and—vengeance ends—the—dreams—of—empire—"

Blood surged from his lips and he died.

"Let me see to your wounds, honorable friend," said Kang Yao, with characteristic Oriental courtesy. "You are bleeding in many places."

"I'm hit in the leg, arm, shoulder and breast-muscles," I grunted. "But nothing serious. But tell me—how did you come here?"

"This one," Kang Yao gestured toward a man in the clothes of a servant. He was the tunnel-keeper and blood was clotted thickly on his temple.

"Yotai Yun shot him," said Kang Yao, "and had him thrown in the river. But the bullet had merely cut a deep groove through his scalp, and the plunge into the water revived him. He got ashore, and thirsting for revenge on his cruel lord, came swiftly to the police and gasped out a tale of plotting and sedition that brought us quickly to the Dragon House. Without, we heard the shots, and burst in quickly. But who lies here in the guise of a Mongolian lama?"

"Rip off his mask," I said, "I'd like to know, myself."

Kang Yao bent and tore off the mask. A startled exclamation escaped him; the skin beneath the mask was neither yellow nor brown. The Black Lama was a white man—Eric Brand!

FANTASY FROM BERKLEY

Robert E. Howard

CONAN: THE HOUR OF THE DRAGON   (03608-1—$1.95)

CONAN: THE PEOPLE OF THE BLACK CIRCLE   (03609-X—$1.95)

CONAN: RED NAILS   (03610-3—$1.95)

MARCHERS OF VALHALLA   (03702-9—$1.95)

SKULL-FACE   (03708-8—$1.95)

* * * * * * *

THONGOR AND THE WIZARD OF LEMURIA
  by Lin Carter   (03435-6—$1.25)

THE SWORDS TRILOGY
  by Michael Moorcock   (03468-2—$1.95)